Sayo

Superintendent Dobbs said, "There weren't any bombs on board and no hijackers. No attempt was made to take over the plane or interfere with it mechanically in any way."

Feiffer said, "I don't quite—"

Dobbs said, "I was the first person on board when the plane landed." He said, "Some of them had been thrown about by the impact of landing." He said, "Others hadn't. Some of the others were still in their seats." He said, "All fifty-seven of them." He paused.

Dobbs said, "They were all dead."

▼   ▼   ▼   ▼

THIN AIR

THIN AIR

A Yellowthread Street Mystery

William Leonard
Marshall

THE MYSTERIOUS PRESS

New York • London • Tokyo

PR
9619.3
M275
T45
1988

MYSTERIOUS PRESS EDITION

This Mysterious Press Edition is published by arrangement with Henry
Holt and Company, Inc., 521 Fifth Avenue, New York, N.Y. 10175

Cover design by George Corsillo

Mysterious Press books are published in association with
Warner Books, Inc.
666 Fifth Avenue
New York, N.Y. 10103
A Warner Communications Company

Printed in the United States of America

First Mysterious Press Printing: August, 1988

10 9 8 7 6 5 4 3 2 1

for Hilary

The Hong Bay district of Hong Kong is fictitious, as are the people who, for one reason or another, inhabit it.

1

Through the half open window of the Detectives' Room in the Yellowthread Street Police Station, Hong Bay, Detective Chief Inspector Harry Feiffer at 9 a.m., feeling fresh, cool, showered and clean-clothed, could feel the crispness of a wonderful Spring day starting. He drew in a nostril of sharp air with a tingle of cold to it and picked up his ringing telephone. The Detectives' Room, for once, was orderly and tidy: there was no one else there. Detective Senior Inspector O'Yee was off somewhere taking infinite pains to teach one of the Chinese desk Constables how to brew a pot of American coffee, Detective Inspector Spencer was out of the office with Detective Inspector Auden investigating a nice lazy call about odd smells somewhere in Canton Street and, generally, all was right with the world. Feiffer said, 'Yes?' pleasantly into the telephone in English.

A voice said back in Cantonese, 'Is that the senior officer?' and Feiffer said just as lazily (taking in another whiff of the Alpine air) in Cantonese, 'That's right.' He took in another breath. A medley of voices went past in the street outside the window. Someone in the group laughed, and then, following the voices, there was a kettledrum tap-tap-tap as slim Chinese girls on high heels hurried towards the shops or work. A long way out in the harbour, a ship's whistle blew to signal sampan owners to come alongside to transfer passengers or light cargo, and a warm smell of hot chestnuts came in as a chestnut seller went by pushing his cart. The smell of the coffee percolating drifted in from somewhere out near the front desk. Feiffer arched his back torpidly. The caller was taking a long time to get to the point. There was no hurry. The caller was muttering about being an emissary and pointing out that even though, technically, he only represented someone else, that wasn't to say that he didn't accept a full role in the proceedings and that . . .

Feiffer thought it was the sort of day to take a long, lazy time to get to the point. He arched his back again and said, 'Fine.' He said suddenly into the telephone, 'You must be joking!' He sat up straight.

The caller said, 'I repeat, my Principal and I have determined that the goods utilised in our first transaction shall be of fair average quality standard only.' He said, 'I am his Number Two. The use of high quality merchandise at this stage of the negotiations was felt, mainly by him, I must admit, to be wasteful. So, in concert, a decision was reached to utilise Japanese materials only.' He said, 'In fairness to your well-known acumen and to my own position, I shall now hang up and call you back within a few moments on another number.' He said politely, 'Wait please.'

The line went dead. Feiffer said into the mute instrument—

The phone on O'Yee's desk rang. Number Two's voice said, 'Ah. The actual number of items to be used has been left open since it is merely the demonstration which is cogent. In any event, it is a charter flight organised by Hong Kong Airlines, final destination Tokyo, Japan, which departed at seven fifty-five a.m.' He said, 'My Principal and I would estimate the demonstration to take place sometime within the next fifteen minutes.' There was a brief pause. 'Fourteen minutes, thirty three seconds. I repeat, there is a lethal device on board the aircraft. There is no chance of its being located.' He said blandly, 'I'll ring back at a later stage.' He said quietly, with a trace of pride in his voice, 'My Principal and I have thought of everything.' He said urbanely, 'I wish you a pleasant morning.' He gave Feiffer the number of Kai Tak Airport Security. He said pleasantly, 'It'll save you looking it up.'

Then he was gone.

*

Considerably less than happily, on the corner of Stamford Road and Canton Street, Auden clambered into a pair of grimy blue overalls. He looked down into the open manhole between the two Chinese sewer workers. He looked at Spencer. He looked at Spencer's overalls. He looked down again into the open manhole. He said suddenly to one of the sewer workers, 'Why the hell can't you get your own people to do this sort of thing?' He said to Spencer, 'Well, why the hell can't they?' He said to Spencer, 'Well? Aye?'

The first sewer worker, an ancient grizzled looking individual in brown overalls (at least, they were brown now) moved his head to look at the younger, second sewer worker. The mere transference of the angle of his head in space released a sudden mortal aroma of vintage sewer.

Auden said, 'Don't move! Just stand there and tell me without moving!' He said to Spencer with feeling, 'God!'

The first sewer worker stood still. He moved his mouth with careful little movements. He said between gritted teeth, 'Can't get people to—'

Auden said, 'Don't you people ever *wash*?' He said again to Spencer, 'God!'

Spencer said, 'Come on, Phil—' He said consolingly in Cantonese to the first worker, 'He's got a very delicate sense of—'

Auden looked into the dark stench of the manhole. He said, 'Why the hell can't you get your own people to go into places like that?' He caught a whiff of sewer worker, 'You two were already down there! Why the hell didn't you have the common decency to go and have a look yourselves?' Something occurred to him, 'And how the hell can you seriously tell the Police there's an odd smell down there?' He snapped at the second sewer worker, 'If this is some sort of bloody clever put-on, you'll find your balls being used for targets in the fastest javelin

3

throw this side of the bloody Moscow Olympics!' He glanced at one or two passers-by who were pressing handkerchiefs to their noses and doing their best to pass by as quickly as possible. He said, 'Got that, have you?'

The second sewer worker nodded. That is to say, he moved. Auden said again, 'Oh—*God*!' He looked at Spencer. He was another of the dumb silent type. Auden said, 'Well? Haven't you got a tongue in your head either?' He said to the first sewer worker, 'And now you're going to tell me that not only can't you two investigate old water channels because you're not with the water people, but that the old water channel is also bloody full of bloody water! Right?'

Spencer said, 'They didn't have to take the trouble to report their suspicions in the first place, Phil, if they—'

'I wish to God they hadn't!' Auden said to the first sewer worker, 'Why the hell don't the water people send their bloody people down?'

The first sewer worker said meekly, 'The two Waterworks men who cover this area are off sick . . .'

'I'm not bloody surprised!!'

Spencer said—

Auden glanced Heavenwards. It was the only direction you could look that didn't have the stink of sewer emanating from it. Auden asked God, 'Why did I want to be a cop in exotic Hong Kong? Why couldn't I have stayed at home in bloody England and done something hygienic like mucking out pig troughs?' He asked God, 'Is there any way I can avoid going down into this stinking bloody hole and finding nothing on this beautiful Spring day when I should be back at the Station watching people brew coffee and stretch their backs?' He asked, 'Well, is there?' He said, 'There isn't.' He said unhappily to the sewer workers, 'Lead on.' He said to Spencer, 'Well, let's get on with it!' He said to the first sewer worker, 'If it's a bloody dead cat in a sack, I'm going to pick it up, attach its tail firmly around your bloody neck, and then I'm going to—'

Spencer said, 'Steady on, Phil—'

Auden said for the third or fourth time, 'God——!'

He followed Spencer and the two sewer workers down into the sewer.

*

Feiffer heard him stifle a snort. Superintendent Dobbs of the Airport Security said, 'Oh, sure.' There was the shattering sound of a jet taking off in the background. It reverberated into Feiffer's ear through the telephone.

Feiffer said, 'I'm not saying it's genuine—'

'Oh good!' Superintendent Dobbs said, 'I'm gratified you're just the tiniest bit impressed by the millions of dollars worth of electronic equipment we've put in out here to avoid just this sort of thing.' He said, 'I'll tell the makers that even down in the bullet-riddled jungle of Hong Bay the drums have told the natives that the Great White Father's magic talks big medicine against the highly sophisticated devices they whip up at nights in their bloody little wigwams and tepees!' He said, 'We don't appreciate bomb hoaxes on Spring days, Feiffer, they're bad for the excursion flights to Hawaiian flower ceremonies.' He said, 'Do you happen to know just how many nuts ring us up to say they've put a hydrogen bomb on Flight Six? *A day*? On average, six or eight. *A day*.' He said, 'And that's only from the *Chinese* schizos. European schizos usually ring up and tell us that there's an electric impulse Venusian ray gun wedged firmly under the shitpan aimed at taking arse samples back into the stratosphere—' He said, 'And that's from the ones who haven't heard the word *biosphere*. For Venusian rays the biosphere is standing room only.' He said, 'Have you ever heard of the Japanese Red Army?' He said, 'Well, the Japanese have and so have we.' He said, 'A charter flight full of bloody Nips rates about as highly here as an El Al flight full of PLO men and Golda Meir.' He said, 'It took two hours for the poor old Japs to even clear body search.' He said,

5

'Let alone the X-raying of freight and luggage.' He said, 'Thanks for the tip, but there isn't any fucking bomb on any flight this fucking day.' He said, 'You've annoyed me suggesting it.'

'He didn't say it was a bomb. He said it was a lethal device.' Feiffer said, 'What am I supposed to do? File it away under Crank?' He said, 'You file it away under Crank.' He said, 'It's your airport, not mine.'

'So why did he ring you and not me?'

'Maybe he thought you'd file it away under Crank.'

'I am going to file it away under Crank!' Dobbs said, 'Do you realise the utter chaos we'd have here if we turned back a plane every time someone rang up and said there was a bomb on board?' He said quickly, 'All right—lethal device.' He said, 'And since the only Japanese charter flight of the day left over an hour ago and the thing on board's supposed to go bang in ten minutes, what the hell am I supposed to do about it?' Dobbs said, 'We get a nice class of people here at the airport. We get nice rich European and American tourists and businessmen and people who can afford to take holidays by jet, and I'm not disrupting everything because some cop from a district I can only describe as a cross between Chicago in the thirties and the Hamburg Reeperbahn at Chinese New Year rings up and tells me some idiot has rung him up.'

'Suit yourself.'

Dobbs paused. He asked quietly, 'Have you looked outside at all today?' He said, 'It's a beautiful Spring day. It's the sort of day when even the Chinese schizos haven't been ringing up because they're out enjoying themselves in the sunshine.' He said, 'Nothing's going to happen to anyone.' He demanded suddenly, 'What's wrong with you people down there?' He said, 'Thanks for the information. I'll file it under Crank with your name on the top copy.' There was another shattering roar as yet another aircraft took off in the background. Dobbs said, 'All right?'

He hung up.

*

Detective Inspector Spencer, a tall, fair-haired shadow in front of Auden said cheerfully over his shoulder, 'I know quite a bit about the Hong Kong sewerage and sanitary systems, as a matter of fact.'

They turned a corner in the dank, flashlight-lit murk. A river of something that smelled indescribable flowed sluggishly by in a cement channel making horrible gurgling noises. Auden did not look at it. He banged his head on a dislodged brick on the roof of the tunnel. He said, 'Do you really?' They turned another corner. The two sewer workers' rubber boots went squelch-glug-squelch on the walkway by the horrible smelling channel.

Spencer said, a little louder, in English, 'I do, actually.' He pointed to something on the curving slimy wall and said happily, 'Chadwick.' He patted the wall affectionately. He called back over his shoulder, 'I read a book about it.' He caressed yet another section of the vile ooze and said for a second time with admiration, 'Chadwick.'

Auden said, 'What's a chadwick?'

'Edwin and Osbert Chadwick. They were the great sanitary pioneers of the nineteenth century.' He noticed something else on the wall and paused, lost in admiration, 'Osbert Chadwick prepared the 1882 Chadwick Report on Hong Kong's sanitary system. There was a competition to design the drains and sewers and when it was won by a clerk in the Public Works Department, Osbert Chadwick came in to do a full and complete study of existing provisions so they could start from there.' He said, 'Edwin Chadwick, on the other hand, was earlier. He was responsible for the sewerage system in England.' He said with awe, 'He was a friend of John Stuart Mill and all sorts of people. He was on the Poor Law Commission.' He called back to Auden, 'You've heard of him, haven't you?'

'I've never heard of either of them. Oswin and who?'

'Os*bert*. Osbert was working in 1880 to about 1910. Edwin died in 1890. He was born in 1801. He was 89 when he died.'

'I'm bloody astounded he lasted so long.' There was a particularly vile something bubbling and flexing away in the centre of the flowing muck. It sounded as if it was fermenting. Auden said, 'If I'd been bloody Edwin down here—'

'Edwin wasn't in these places.' Spencer said patiently, 'Os*bert* was the one who investigated Hong Kong—'

'How long did *he* last?'

'What he found was that there weren't any sewers or drains worth speaking of.'

'Then how long did he bloodywell last when he got round to building a few?' They came to a wider section of the tunnel. There seemed to be faint whiffs of fresh air. Auden shone his flashlight up to the roof to find them. The stench came in to take their place. He heard Spencer ask one of the sewer workers how much longer and the worker reply that they were almost there. Auden said, 'Well, how long did he last?'

The two sewer workers stopped. The first sewer worker indicated a hole in the wall at about knee height that looked as if it had been made with a sledgehammer. The first sewer worker said, 'There.' He said, 'The old water channel's in through there.' He said helpfully, 'There's just enough room to squeeze through.'

Auden said in Cantonese, 'Then why didn't you?'

'Not our section.' The older sewer worker's voice said above the steady meandering of the slime, 'That's Waterworks property.' He said, 'We smelled a funny smell.' He and his partner moved along the walkway to make room for Spencer to squat down.

Spencer put his head into the hole. He made sniffing noises. Auden said, 'Well?'

Spencer stopped sniffing. His head came back out of the hole. 'There is an odd smell.'

Auden said, 'How can you tell?' He went forward and took Spencer's place at the hole. There was a smell. It was familiar.

8

It reminded him of mornings out in the open somewhere.

Spencer said, 'What do you think?' He said, 'It seems familiar, but I can't place it.' He said, 'Somewhere out in the open.'

Auden said, 'Cordite. It smells like a pistol range.' He said curiously, 'It smells like some sort of explosive.' He asked the first sewer worker, 'What's above here?'

The first sewer worker thought for a moment. The idea that there might be things above the sewers had plainly never occurred to him.

Auden said to Spencer, 'It's some sort of nitrate.' He sniffed again. The smell was very strong. He shone his flashlight in and saw layers of blue smoke moving in currents. He said to Spencer, 'Come on, Edwin—' and squeezed in through the hole into the water channel.

Spencer said, '*Osbert—Osbert* was the one in Hong—' He said to the two sewer workers in Cantonese, 'Wait here,' and went in through the hole.

*

Feiffer's phone rang. It was Superintendent Dobbs. Dobbs said, 'Feiffer—?' There was the sound of a jet taking off in the background.

'Yes.'

'What did you do? You had the plane contacted and you ordered it back!' Dobbs shouted above the retreating sound of the jet, 'Who the hell do you think's in charge around here? You don't just ring up someone and have them order a jet back without authority! I'm in charge around here—if anyone rings up people to have jets ordered back, *I* ring up people to have jets ordered back!' He demanded, 'Who did you ring?' He said, 'I'll have you for this!'

'I haven't the faintest idea what you're—'

'The plane's on its way back! The charter flight! What the hell do you know about it?'

'I don't know anything about it!'

'Someone's had the plane turned back to bloody Hong Kong without my authority and at the moment, you strike me as the likeliest bloody candidate by a long shot! You and your bloody seedy little district and your seedy little detectives and your seedy little lethal—what the hell do you know about it?'

'Nothing!'

'Then who ordered it back?'

'How the hell should I know? Why not ask the bloody pilot?'

'The bloody pilot isn't talking! The bloody pilot's making noises over the radio like an old lady who's just been gangbanged by fourteen fucking randy gorillas! The bloody pilot's in a state of shock! What the hell did you tell him?'

'How could I tell him anything?' Feiffer said, 'You listen to me, Dobbs—'

'Superintendent Dobbs to you!'

'Listen, Dobbs, I don't appreciate being shouted at by uniformed Superintendents or anyone else—'

'If you didn't have the plane turned back, then who did? And why?'

'I haven't the faintest idea. Why don't you ask the Tower?'

'The Tower don't know!'

'Then how could I have contacted the plane? By bloody remote control?'

'Pilots don't go into shock over bomb hoaxes. Not unless they're real. According to you, it should have gone off twenty minutes ago—'

'According to my caller.'

'—according to your caller.' Dobbs said, 'Hmm.' He said suddenly, 'I'll ring you back.'

'I can hardly wait.'

Dobbs paused for a moment. He said thoughtfully, 'Yeah. . . .' He said, 'Twenty minutes. . . .' He said, '—by God, Feiffer, if I find out that it was you—' He changed his mind about something.

He said quickly, 'I'll ring you back.'

*

Auden was standing with his back to the water channel with his flashlight switched off. The smell was very strong. It smelled as if a regiment of combat-shooters had let loose with everything they had in one shattering burst. Spencer switched on his flashlight. Layers of heavy blue smoke moved lazily in the ray. He shone the light around in the old water channel. It was silent and arid, waterless. Something tapped against his foot and he shone the light down to see it. It glistened in the light and Spencer picked it up. He examined it. It was a fired nine millimetre rimless cartridge case. He moved the light. There was another case on the concrete floor, its brass gleaming, and then another.

He shone his light up against the far wall. The wall was pocked in rising lines with holes and craters where the bullets from the empty cases had smashed themselves against the brickwork. There were stains on the wall, running down, and here and there, a sunspot of dark liquid in a violent splash. There was the stale moss-cold smell of death.

Auden switched on his flashlight. He moved the light towards a section of the wall. There were little glistening flashes as the beam picked out rows and piles of empty brass cases. Auden said, 'Over there.'

The smell of cordite was intensely strong.

Auden's light moved a few feet to the left.

There were six dead bodies lying in a row against the wall. They were were all naked and covered in blood. Around them, like offerings, were more rows of the little brass cases and, behind them on the wall, lines of more craters and pocks on the wall where the bullets had gone after they had finished killing.

Spencer began counting the holes in the wall automatically. He got to twenty-nine and stopped. He began counting the cases on the floor. He reached forty-seven and there were still more.

Auden said, 'Two magazines from a fully automatic weapon.' He said evenly, 'Maybe more?' All the corpses were male, Chinese, and in their mid forties and fifties. They were all totally naked.

Auden said, 'Someone brought them down here, made them undress, lined them up against the wall and then machine-gunned them.'

Spencer nodded.

Auden said, 'Well . . .' He switched off his flashlight. The corpses in a row, silent and still, in the yellow light from the two flashlights, looked like a row of emaciated dead goldfish in a waterless glass tank.

Auden said quietly, 'What a way to die.'

He went towards the hole in the wall carefully, so as not to disturb anything.

*

There was a long pause, then Dobbs said for the second time, 'Chief Inspector Feiffer?'

'Yes—?'

Dobbs said, 'The flight is back. I've just been on board to search it for bombs and to talk to the pilot.' He said in an odd voice, 'The pilot's been taken to hospital suffering from shock.' Dobbs said, 'There were four crew and fifty-seven passengers on the plane. The fifty-seven passengers were Japanese businessmen and their wives who'd been in Hong Kong on a shopping expedition organised by their local businessmen's club.' He said, 'The charter had been organised by Hong Kong airlines to fill one of their smaller aircraft that used to be on the Hong Kong–Taipei run before the Boeings took over.' He said, 'There weren't any bombs on board and no hijackers. No attempt was made to take over the plane or interfere with it mechanically in any way.' He said, 'My people are taking statements from the crew and we'll get something from the pilot later today when he's recovered.' He said, 'My people will be down to see you later this morning so I'd be grateful if you'd keep yourself available.'

'All right.'

'—that's very good of you.' He sounded a long way off.

Feiffer said, 'What about the passengers?'

There was another pause. Dobbs said, 'The passengers?'

'Yes.'

Dobbs said, 'The pilot flew back with the crew locked in with him in his cabin. When the plane landed no one had the courage to go back into the passengers' section to strap the passengers in.' He said quietly, 'I was the first person on board when the aircraft landed.'

Feiffer said, 'I don't quite—'

Dobbs said, 'I found them.' He said, 'Some of them had been thrown about by the impact of landing.' He said, 'Others hadn't. Some of the others were still in their seats.' He said, 'All fifty-seven of them.' He paused.

Dobbs said, 'They were all dead.'

2

Feiffer said into the phone, 'O.K., if the Scientific people are finished then you'd better both go down to the Morgue with the bodies.' He paused and made a note of the times on a report sheet. He said into the phone, '... yes ... fine ...' Two large shadows fell across his desk and he looked up. 'Call me back when you're down there and we'll ...' He said, 'Fine, O.K.'

He hung up and looked at the shadows. The shadows were of two immaculately turned out and uniformed policemen, one European and the other Chinese. He glanced at O'Yee. O'Yee gazed at the ceiling.

The European policeman said, 'Chief Inspector Munday, Kai Tak.'

The Chinese said, 'Inspector Ming.'

They waited, gleaming.

Feiffer glanced again at O'Yee. O'Yee's eyes cemented themselves into the ceiling. He seemed to be smiling. Feiffer said, 'Yes?'

Munday said, 'Detective Chief Inspector Feiffer?'

'Yes.'

Ming said to O'Yee, 'And you are?'

O'Yee kept his eyes on the ceiling. 'Senior Detective Inspector O'Yee.'

Ming said, 'Oh.' He looked back to Feiffer.

Feiffer said, 'Sit down.'

Munday said, 'We prefer to stand.' He brushed a speck of dust from his starched shirt cuff without looking down. How a brown-haired European with green eyes and a black-haired Chinese with brown eyes could look almost identical was something Feiffer thought he'd have to ask the Identikit people about. They even sounded the same. Ming's English was accentless. Munday said, 'We've come about your informant.' He said, 'We want the rest of the information.' He glanced down at the knife-edge crease in his trousers and looked satisfied.

'There isn't any rest of the information. I gave it all to your senior officer.'

Inspector Ming said, 'To—?'

Feiffer said, 'Dobbs.'

Chief Inspector Munday said, 'Superintendent Dobbs.' He looked at the walls of the room significantly. They were stained and peeling. They needed a good coat of paint. Munday said, 'And?'

'And nothing. I told him everything I knew. There isn't anything else to tell. The man rang up calling himself Number Two and muttered something about his Principal and some sort of business transaction, and then he told me he'd done something to a charter flight. He used two telephones so the call couldn't be traced.'

Chief Inspector Munday glanced at Feiffer's telephone. The receiver was cracked. He raised an eyebrow. He asked critically, 'Did you attempt to trace it?'

'At the time, no. I assumed—as did your Mr Dobbs—that it was probably just a crank call.' He said seriously, 'It wasn't, was it?'

Munday had one of those faces that looked like it had been cast in one piece out of fast-setting cement. It showed nothing. Munday said from thin lips that hardly appeared to move, 'No.'

Feiffer said, 'I'm very sorry, but that's all I know. How did the passengers die?'

Inspector Ming asked, 'Any idea why he chose to call you rather than us?'

'Maybe he just wasn't used to dealing with a better class of people.'

Munday said, 'Hmm.' He glanced around the room and the two so-called police officers who occupied it. He said for the second time, 'Hmm.'

Feiffer said, 'Apart from asking me bloody stupid questions, what are you people doing about it?'

Munday said quickly, 'We've got the matter in hand. Interviews with the appropriate people are taking place at this very moment.' He added hurriedly, 'I refer to appropriate people at Kai Tak. We have a fair idea where the actual mechanics of the thing took place and it's only a matter of finding the accomplices.' He said dismissively, 'They'll be found at Kai Tak.' He said, 'You could do one thing for us to save us going through channels to get permission to take interviews in your district, and that's go and talk to someone for us in Tiger Snake Road.' He said encouragingly, 'It's only a routine enquiry otherwise we'd do it ourselves.' He said thoughtfully, 'That is, if you want to feel part of the business—'

'He did ring me, after all.'

Munday said earnestly, 'How can you people work in a place like this?' He looked about the room, 'In a place like Hong Bay?'

Munday said, 'All the bloodshed and mayhem you people seem to collect down here—' He said to Ming, 'Well, you were posted here yourself once, weren't you?'

Inspector Ming nodded. The phone on O'Yee's desk rang and he watched O'Yee answer it.

O'Yee said into the phone, 'Oh . . . right . . .' He paused, listening.

Chief Inspector Munday said to Feiffer, 'Another mass slaughter with the meat cleavers?'

Feiffer smiled wanly. He watched O'Yee on the phone.

O'Yee said, '. . . yes . . . O.K. Call us back then . . . O.K. Sure . . . I'll pass it on . . .' He said quietly in his soft San Franciscan accent, 'Just take it slowly and maybe it won't seem so bad . . .' He said, 'Fine. Right,' and hung up. He looked across at Feiffer and said, 'Bill Spencer ringing from the Morgue. He and Auden are out there now with the bodies. They'll get in touch when the police photographer's done a few head and shoulders ID shots.' He smiled insincerely at Inspector Ming.

Chief Inspector Munday shook his head. He flicked another speck of grime from his uniform. He said, 'Bodies—' He asked Feiffer, 'Another gang war with the razors out? Or was it a few hand grenades or mortar bombs in the main shopping precinct?' He asked, 'Just as a matter of interest, what is the body count in Hong Bay up to today?' He asked, 'Twenty? Twenty-five?'

Feiffer said, 'Six.' He glanced at O'Yee. He said to Munday pleasantly. 'Wrong on all counts. No razors, cleavers or mortar bombs.' He said evenly, 'As a matter of fact, they were machine-gunned.' He waited for Munday and Ming, sartorically splendidly laundered the pair of them, to exchange significant nods.

There was a brief pause.

Significant nods were exchanged.

*

Hong Kong is an island of some 30 square miles under British administration in the South China Sea facing the Kowloon and New Territories areas of continental China. Kowloon and the New Territories are also British administered, surrounded by the Communist Chinese province of Kwantung. The climate is generally sub-tropical, with hot, humid summers and heavy rainfall. The population of Hong Kong and the surrounding areas at any one time, including tourists and visitors, is in excess of four million. The New Territories are leased from the Chinese. The lease is due to expire in 1997, but the British nevertheless maintain a military presence along the border, although, should the Communists, who supply almost all the Colony's drinking water, ever desire to terminate the lease early, they need only turn off the taps. Hong Bay is on the southern side of the island and the tourist brochures advise you not to go there after dark.

*

The autopsy room in the mortuary was attached to the St Paul de Chartres' hospital on Hong Bay Beach Road. There was a single opaque skylight in the centre of the roof and strip heating on the white tiled walls. Notices in English and Chinese listed the standard procedures for checking bodies in and out, what to do in the event of decapitated or legless corpses (place the additional sections of anatomy in plastic receptacles alongside the trunk), and the appropriate temperatures at which to run the freezers in all seasons. Another notice, added to in various coloured pens and ballpoints, gave the names of undertakers authorised to pick up and deliver.

A final notice warned that pilfering from the pockets of the dead was a criminal offence.

There was a stainless steel post-mortem tray in the centre of the room with an operating table with a drain hole in it at one end, and to one side of it, a bookcase affair for instruments including a surgical circular saw for cases where the pathologist might want to examine the deceased's brain. The entire place: the walls, freezers, floor, table, instruments and cranium circular saw, smelled of Lysol.

Auden opened one of the stainless steel freezers. Facing him in two vertical rows were six pairs of bare feet. Around the ankles of each was a strip of wide adhesive tape binding them together. Each of the strips had the same legend written on it in ink: UNIDENTIFIED CHINESE MALE (POLICE). The strips were marked 1 to 6. The interior of the freezer smelled cold and disinfected. The feet looked like pale rubber. There were calluses and corns on some of the soles and insteps.

Auden glanced at Spencer. Doctor Macarthur came in from a side door and shook his head.

Auden said, 'Well?'

Macarthur shook his head. He asked Spencer, 'Do you know how to use a lifter?' He nodded to a machine to one side of the freezer that looked like a steel stretcher with a hydraulic jack and a rubber-wheeled trolley attached to it. He said to Spencer, 'You just jack it up to the level of the tray you want in the freezer, slide the tray out with the body on, run it onto the lifter, pull the lifter back, jack it down again, and *voilà*, one body at the required height from the ground.' He said, 'The bodies you want are numbered one to six. Do them in that order.' He said, 'Put them back in the same tidy order as you found them.'

Spencer said, 'Do we have to do the photos ourselves?' He glanced back into the freezer.

'Afraid so. All the police photographers are evidently fully engaged at Kai Tak.' Macarthur said, 'Still, you only want a few for your own use.' He said, 'There's a Polaroid camera on the instrument shelves next to the set of rib cutters. Use that.' He said, 'I may have to go out to Kai Tak myself if the Japanese give clearance for autopsies so you'd better get started right away.' He said, 'When you take the photos, it might be an idea for one of you to hold the dead man's mouth closed, provided rigor mortis hasn't advanced.' He said, 'You do it with a firm upward pressure of the heel of your hand. It looks less dead when you come to show the pictures around. If rigor mortis has started to set in, you'll have to push fairly hard.' He said, 'Please be careful not to break the jaw.' He asked, 'Is everything clear?'

Spencer nodded. He looked at Auden. Spencer said, 'I'll hold the mouth closed.'

'You've done it before?'

Spencer shook his head.

'Good experience for you then.' He cast a quick glance at the freezer. 'Gangsters, were they?'

Spencer shrugged.

'I can see why you want the photos. If they're gangsters, you can show them around the appropriate dives. Right?'

Auden nodded.

Macarthur grinned. He said, 'Dives—' He was a tall, white-coated individual with a Roman nose. He had a French cigarette in his mouth, unlit. Macarthur said, 'That's how they talk.' He said happily, 'I would have made a good detective.'

Auden said, 'Two of the bodies took bullets in the head—'

Macarthur nodded. He remembered his cigarette and took out a lighter. The lighter refused to function. Auden lit the cigarette for him with a match. Macarthur said, 'Oh, just cover that part of the skull with the sheet.' He drew in deeply on the cigarette. 'Or if the section shot away is on the face you could cover it with a piece of adhesive plaster.' He said, 'In any event, I'll leave it to you to work out for yourselves. I have to get back to Pathology to start making out the preliminary forms for the autopsies.'

Auden said, 'What autopsies?'

'On the six corpses, of course.' Macarthur looked slightly shocked. He said, 'Naturally, when you've finished taking all the photos you have to be present for the post-mortems.' He said, surprised, 'I thought you both realised that. We have to do the PMs and the fingerprinting.' Macarthur said, 'It's standard procedure.' He glanced at the plethora of wall notices meaningfully. 'Naturally, we have to find out exactly how they died.'

Auden said, 'They were bloody shot!' He glanced at the stainless steel lifter. He looked at Spencer.

Spencer said quietly, 'Do we really have to be present for—'

Macarthur grinned at Spencer to encourage him. 'I'll leave you to get on with your pictures.' He glanced at Spencer for the second time. He said encouragingly, 'Once you get the hang of it you'll find it absolutely fascinating.' He drew on his cigarette and nodded to himself. He said thoughtfully, '. . . really fascinating . . .'

He said, 'I'll leave you to get on with it.'

Munday and Ming still stood.

Chief Inspector Munday said, 'They were poisoned.' He said, 'As far as we can ascertain externally, with some sort of cyanide.' He said, 'The Japanese authorities aren't being very co-operative at the moment in the matter of post-mortems, but we expect some action in the next few hours. Inasmuch as our experts have only been allowed a cursory examination, it was some sort of industrial or medical pure-strength compound that makes death virtually instantaneous.' He said grandly, 'Cyanide attacks the respiratory system, in case you didn't know.'

Feiffer glanced at him.

'You did know that?'

Feiffer said, 'I always thought it was the intra-cellular system.' He asked, 'How was it administered?'

Munday said, 'Well, whatever. I'm sure you people have had more experience of poisoners than we have.' He said, 'It was in the pre-packaged food served for the morning meal in flight. Inserted by a hypodermic needle and then the hole in the covering foil resealed with some sort of rubber compound.' He said, 'Like a self-sealing tyre. The aircraft carried eighty prepared meals as standard. They served fifty-seven of them. It took a microscope to detect the holes where the needle had gone in.' He said, 'We think it may be some sort of prussic acid solution and that the holes were sealed to stop it evaporating.'

Feiffer said, 'Or killing the cabin staff. Prussic kills by inhalation as well as ingestion.' He glanced at the surface of his desk and brushed away an imaginary speck of dust.

Munday said irritably, 'Well, whatever! The fact of the matter is that we've got a fair idea that the job was done by one of the food handlers at the airport and we've roped the whole bloody lot of them in for questioning!' He said, exasperated, to Ming, 'Right?'

Inspector Ming said, 'Yes, sir.'

Chief Inspector Munday said, 'It's only a matter of time until one of them breaks down and admits it and then we've got his boss as well.'

Inspector Ming said, 'Your caller.'

'My caller referred to himself as Number Two. That tends to suggest to my simple mind that he isn't the boss, but that someone else is.'

Munday said, 'Poppycock!'

Feiffer glanced down at the surface of his desk.

Munday said, irritably, 'In any event, the food is pre-cooked and packaged here in Hong Kong. In Tiger Snake Road, to be precise, number 45A. We'd like you to go out there and talk to the man in charge and make sure he knows nothing about it just for the record.' Munday said, 'Could you possibly bring yourselves to perform that simple task? Or isn't it gory and exciting enough for you?'

Feiffer did not reply.

Munday said with feeling, 'You people make me sick! You people give the police a bad name with all this emphasis on blood and bloody violence!' He said, 'Why the hell can't you people in areas like this just try to calm down a little? Do you have to go charging about day and night all the bloody time with bloody psychos and goddamned maniacs? Why the hell can't you people make it easy on everyone and just—'

O'Yee said, 'Get ourselves posted to Kai Tak?'

'Well, why the hell not?'

Feiffer said evenly, 'We'll go and see your food packager and let you know what he says.'

'Thank you very much! And see if you can do it, would you, without too much mayhem?' Munday slapped his tunic, 'I don't even carry a gun!' He glanced at O'Yee in his shirt-sleeves and upside-down Burns-Martin speed holster and demanded, 'Just what the hell's that supposed to be? Bloody Eliot Ness?' He said, disgusted, 'Six people machine-gunned!' He said, 'I don't know why some civilised person doesn't just fill the local water supply with arsenic or something and get rid of the whole bloody lot of you?' He had gone red in the face. He looked at Feiffer.

O'Yee said, 'The civilised person probably used up all his cyanide killing fifty-seven people at Kai Tak.' He said evenly, 'Still if there's any left, and you ever catch him, maybe you can give him our address.'

'Just see you talk to the food packers and keep my people well out of your slimy little district and you'll be doing more than enough to keep everyone happy, Senior Inspector! All right?'

O'Yee said, 'Yes, *sir*!' He winced as the door slammed shut and glanced at Feiffer. Feiffer took his Detective Special .38 from his desk drawer and clipped it into his holster. He seemed about to say something.

He changed his mind and rang down for a car.

*

Outside the Mortuary, Spencer watched Auden add a line to the entry in his notebook. Spencer swallowed. It was mid afternoon. They had been in the Mortuary for over four hours. He swallowed again.

Auden closed the notebook and flipped through the photographs. They were of very poor quality. He looked up to Spencer and passed half of them over. Auden said, 'Now we check Fingerprints and Missing Persons at Headquarters and then if we get nothing we start legging it about showing people pretty postcards.' He heard a sound behind him and turned to see Macarthur sliding the Mortuary door shut and searching in his pocket for the key.

Macarthur said, 'The Japanese authorities have given their permission.' He said to Auden, 'There'll be P.M.s on the passengers going on virtually non-stop until tomorrow night.' He said cheerfully to Auden, 'It's been a truly interesting day all round.' He locked the padlock on the Morgue and started for the carpark.

Auden said, 'Truly fascinating.'

Spencer said, 'Truly terrific.'

He sounded, just for a moment, Macarthur thought, exactly like Auden.

*

Dobbs said irritably down the line, 'What the hell's that noise? It sounds like you're ringing me from the middle of a bloody horn honking contest!'

Feiffer said, 'I'm ringing from near the fish markets off Tiger Snake Road.' There was a profusion of honking, shouting, cursing and meshing of gears as yet another three trucks fought and hooted their way around the corner into Beach Road. They were laden with fruit and vegetables for the open air restaurants and foodstalls, roped precariously in terrifyingly fragile mountains and towers of wooden boxes and rattan baskets. A Dodge truck carrying a load of live chickens almost collided with one of the vegetable trucks—an even more ancient Ford—and the driver got out armed with a tyre iron to mash a few vegetables. The honking from in front and behind the chicken truck intensified, and then the honking from behind the vegetable truck replied in kind. The chicken driver took a swing at something on the vegetable driver's truck—one of his rear tyres—and pointed out graphically that if anyone was stupid enough to drive a truck of that width around a corner the width of Tiger Snake Road then he deserved to have someone driving a thinner, more sensible chicken truck whack his rear tyres with a tyre iron. Feiffer said, 'I've seen the food packaging people. I thought you'd want to know straight away.' He shouted above the din, 'I saw the owner. Apparently the packaging is done in the evenings to keep the stuff fresh for the next day. No one turns up until about six at night.'

'Then what was he doing there in the middle of the afternoon?'

'He was giving orders to his writer and working out the accounts.' There was a cacophony of honking and cursing. The vegetable truck driver decided he might just smash the chicken truck driver's face in. He reached into his cab for a tyre iron like the chicken driver's and came out with a bigger one. He looked at it in happy surprise. The chicken driver looked at his own tyre iron. He nodded to his mate in his cab. His mate came out of the cab carrying a crowbar. The vegetable man nodded, in turn, to his cab. His mate came out carrying an axe.

O'Yee got out of the car outside the phone booth and began to go towards the trucks. A uniformed Constable appeared from behind a truck carrying a load of melons and began to go unhurriedly towards the combatants. He blew a piercing blast on his whistle and both the combatants turned around. Crowbars, tyre irons and axes disappeared as if by magic. O'Yee got back into the car.

Dobbs shouted down the line. 'Are you still there?'

'The owner is an ex-butcher. He's had the business for about six years, supplying pre-cooked and packaged foods to Hong Kong Airlines and one of the tour companies that runs all-day excursions to the outlying islands. The premises are on two floors. The meals are cooked downstairs in the kitchen, then packed into little cartons as individual servings covered with airtight aluminum foil, then stored away in freezers until they're picked up by a contract trucking firm based at the airport at about four or five o'clock in the morning.'

'We know about the trucking firm.'

'And?'

Dobbs said, 'It's just some local Chink set-up. It's in hand. Anything else?' Dobbs said, 'Who did you say was there with him? With the owner?'

'His writer.'

'His what?'

Feiffer said, 'The owner is an ex-butcher.'

'So?'

'So he's lost quite a few fingers along the way. And both his thumbs. He can't write. He employs a scribe to enter his accounts and write orders down for him.'

'Another bloody illiterate—'

Feiffer glanced across at the junction of Tiger Snake Road. The chicken man and the vegetable man had their arms around each other's shoulders. The way they were telling it to the Constable, they had been friends for life and had merely stopped in a welter of brotherly love to renew their fraternal devotion. The axe, tyre iron and the crowbar? What axe, tyre iron and crowbar? Feiffer said wearily, 'He isn't illiterate. He's just lost two or three fingers. The food is picked up in the early morning and checked off by the owner and his scribe. By that time the owner, scribe and one or two cleaners are the only people still there.' He said, 'The owner showed me a few of his contracts. He seems to be doing very well. And if he can't use his hands to write a few characters then he certainly couldn't use them for anything as delicate as filling a hypo and sliding it into a piece of aluminium foil.'

'What's he like? This owner?'

'Middle-aged Cantonese. Bald. Pot-bellied and prosperous. The premises are clean and moderately capitalised. Two large freezers for the food, padlocked, and double locks on the other doors. O'Yee checked the burglar alarm system. It's basic but effective. The owner is a man making money and enjoying it. In fact, he's just bought a Mercedes. I rang the firm who sold it to him. He paid cash, but only after he'd brought the price down fifteen per cent by two hours hard bargaining. Generally, I'd say he wasn't above short-weighing a bit here and there on his food, but other than that he struck me as very respectable.'

'And the scribe?'

'The scribe is an old man from the old Chinese scholar class. He must be eighty or eighty-five years old if he's a day. Maybe older.' Feiffer said, 'If it was so important to Munday's case, maybe he should have spoken to the owner and the scribe himself. I'm not even certain what I'm supposed to be looking for.' Feiffer said, 'Munday gave the impression that it was just routine. Why is it worth all this long discussion?' He asked, 'Is it important for some reason?'

26

The vegetable man and the chicken man began an orgy of back-slapping and cameraderie for the benefit of the uniformed Constable. The uniformed Constable looked far from convinced. The vegetable man pointed to the cab of his truck beseechingly. He pointed to his wrist. He didn't seem to be wearing a watch. He looked at his old friend the chicken man. The chicken man did have a watch. It was a mere nothing for the chicken man to pass over his watch so his old friend the vegetable man might satisfy his curiosity about the time. His old friend the vegetable man showed the time to the uniformed Constable and pointed significantly to his load. The Constable still looked far from convinced. The uniformed Constable nodded and indicated the vegetable man's truck, then ordered the chicken truck man back to his truck as well and went to the centre of the road to direct traffic. The chicken man waved to the uniformed Constable thankfully. He waved to his old friend the vegetable truck man. The traffic in front of the two trucks began moving. The chicken truck driver waved to the traffic.

Dobbs said, 'The truth is we're not getting very far with our enquiries at Kai Tak.'

'No?' Feiffer watched the uniformed Constable in action. His signals were a joy to watch. The chicken man and the vegetable man both looked relieved. You could have been in big trouble with a cop who could give traffic signals with the authority and grace of a ballet dancer. They both breathed sighs of survival.

Dobbs said, 'Are you absolutely certain that the owner couldn't have been the one who did it?'

'I formed the impression that he was hard working and respectable. He seemed very surprised to see me.'

'You didn't tell him what happened?'

'No, I didn't tell him what happened. He seemed surprised to get a visit from the cops, that's all. If he'd just engineered the deaths of a planeload of people then he was very calm about it.' Feiffer said, 'I'm sorry, but it looks like you're not going to get anything from this end either.'

'The owner wasn't the man who rang you? This Number Two character?'

'No.'

'Why did Number Two ring you in the first place? Instead of someone else?'

'I've no idea. As I told Munday. Is he back yet? Munday?'

'He's back.'

The traffic directly in front of the chicken truck began to move. The chicken truck driver started his engine and cast a quick glance at the vegetable truck driver. The vegetable truck driver cast a quick glance at him. The uniformed Constable cast a quick glance at the pair of them. The vegetable truck driver and the chicken truck driver smiled at each other effusively.

Feiffer said, 'I'm sorry, but that's all I know. What you haven't told me yet is why all those people were killed.'

There was a pause. Dobbs said, 'We don't know why.' He said quietly, 'Well, thanks anyway.'

The vegetable man's truck drew level with the chicken man's truck and passed it. Both the chicken man and the vegetable man waved to each other happily.

Feiffer said, 'If there's anything else we can do to help, we will, but the fact is he probably just picked out the first Police Station he found in the telephone book and rang it. As for this transaction business, I don't know what he meant at all.' He said, 'Maybe the next time—if there is a next time—he'll ring Kai Tak direct and—'

Dobbs said, 'I don't need to be patronised by you, Feiffer!'

The chicken man's truck began to move away. He watched his old friend the vegetable man's truck begin to turn the corner. The chicken man wondered whether he was going to be late. He glanced at his watch.

Dobbs said, 'To hell with you!' He hung up.

The chicken man shrieked to the uniformed Constable. 'Him! Him!' He stabbed his finger in the direction of the disappearing vegetable truck.

The Constable looked around.

The chicken man shrieked emphatically, 'That bastard's stolen my watch!' He gunned the motor of his truck and reached down for his tyre iron.

*

The bland voice at the other end of the telephone said, 'Ah. I rang earlier, but you were out. I'm glad I caught you. Oblige me if you would by keeping yourself available for the next few moments while I change to another telephone in order to keep our transaction on a plane of mutual trust and respect.' He asked pleasantly, 'Would you do that please, Mr Feiffer?'

Feiffer did not reply.

Number Two said, 'Thank you.'

The line went dead.

3

Feiffer said urgently to O'Yee, 'Use my telephone. Get Superintendent Dobbs on the line—quickly'. The phone on O'Yee's desk rang and Feiffer snatched it up.

O'Yee said, 'Him?' and Feiffer nodded. O'Yee began dialling the number for Kai Tak.

There was a pause (there were no background noises), and then Number Two's voice said unhurriedly in Cantonese, 'Feiffer Sin Sang a?'

'Hai.'

Number Two said in Cantonese, 'I like dealing with reliable associates. The question of money, as you will have already realised, should, by rights, be broached at this stage of our negotiations.' He asked, 'That has occurred to you of course?' He asked a little warily, 'Surely you did not imagine that a demonstration of such effectiveness was simply the work of someone who had nothing in mind more commercial than to see his name in the newspapers?' He said, 'No. You realised that it was a business transaction.'

O'Yee said into his phone, 'Superintendent Dobbs?'

'This is Dobbs.'

O'Yee said, 'We've got Number Two on the other line.' He gave Dobbs the other number, 'If I tell you to hang up and ring on the other line, then do it. He keeps changing lines so we can't trace it.'

Dobbs said, 'Tell the little sod to ring me direct!' There was no trace of argument in his voice.

30

Feiffer said to Number Two, 'What I don't understand is why you think I should be able to negotiate any deal between you and the authorities.' He saw O'Yee making stabbing and dialling motions at his telephone with his finger, 'The people for you to speak to are at Kai Tak.'

There was a pause.

O'Yee said to Dobbs, 'He's told him.'

' And?'

Number Two said, 'No.'

'Why not?'

There was another pause.

O'Yee said into his phone, 'He refuses.' He glanced at Feiffer. Feiffer shook his head. O'Yee said, 'He says no.'

'Why not?'

O'Yee mouthed at Feiffer, '*Why not?*'

Number Two said, 'Superintendent Dobbs is the person at Kai Tak. Market research was done on him before it was done on you.' Number Two said, 'Do you know that Dobbs has only reached the minimum elementary stage in Cantonese required by the Government after being in the Colony for more than eighteen years?' He asked Feiffer as one Cantonese-speaker to another, 'That's not much to recommend him, is it?' There was another brief pause (Feiffer wondered what he was doing), and then Number Two said, 'And apart from that, I don't like the look of him.' There was another, shorter stop.

Dobbs said to O'Yee, 'Well?'

Number Two said, 'Time's up.'

O'Yee looked at Feiffer.

Feiffer's line went dead.

Dobbs said, 'Well? What does he—'

O'Yee said, 'Hang up. Ring the other number.' He put the phone down a second before it started ringing again. He handed it to Feiffer and then went to answer his own.

Number Two said, 'Who was on the other line?'

'My partner, Senior Inspector O'Yee.'

'Talking to whom?'

Feiffer paused. He heard O'Yee say into the other phone, 'I don't *know* why! He just said no!'

Feiffer said, 'Mr O'Yee was talking to Superintendent Dobbs at Kai Tak.'

Dobbs said, 'He told him? Is he out of his *mind*?'

Feiffer said, 'Mr Dobbs was insistent that you ring him direct and I told him I'd pass on your message. I have.' Feiffer said, 'I'm working on the assumption that you have a second lethal device at your disposal and that if I cross you you're quite capable of setting it off as yet another demonstration. Another demonstration isn't necessary.'

Dobbs said to O'Yee, 'Good God in Heaven, what the hell does he think security is all about! If there's another device we'd have found it!' He said to someone standing next to him at the phone, 'Good fucking God in Heaven!'

There was a silence from Number Two's end of the phone. Number Two said, 'I regret the necessity to keep changing telephones, but having researched the correlation between your desire to keep your word, Mr Feiffer, and your urge to catch criminals it seems a small precaution for which you may probably forgive me.' He waited.

Feiffer said, 'I forgive you.'

Dobbs said, 'Well? Well? What's happening?'

O'Yee said, 'Harry's forgiving him.'

There was a terrible silence from Kai Tak.

Number Two said, 'You're quite correct about the second device. My Principal has determined that it should be set in action against the eventuality that the authorities may not desire to bring our transaction to an immediate and mutually satisfactory conclusion.' He said, 'My Principal is very perceptive about these things and it is his feeling that the necessity of another demonstration is in the order of sixty-five percent statistical possibility.' He said, 'You may inform Mr Dobbs on the other line, therefore, that another device has been set and that he has missed it.'

32

Feiffer said to O'Yee, 'Tell Dobbs that another device has been set. Tell him it's probably already in the air.'

Number Two said, 'It *is* in the air.'

'Tell Dobbs it's on a flight that's already left.' Feiffer asked, 'So what do you want? In terms of money?'

Dobbs shouted, 'Balls!' Feiffer heard it from O'Yee's telephone clear across the room.

Number Two said, 'One hundred thousand U.S. dollars in denominations no larger than twenties.'

'And presumably not in running serial numbers.'

Dobbs shouted, 'Balls! It's bloody balls!'

Number Two said, 'I don't care one way or the other.'

'You don't care whether the numbers are running?'

Number Two said, 'No.'

O'Yee passed on the information. There was a silence from Kai Tak. Dobbs said, 'It's a hoax. There isn't a device.'

Feiffer said to Number Two, 'Which flight is the device on?'

'The money is to be delivered by you personally at the old bus depot on the corner of Peking Road, in the number three repair shed at six o'clock this evening.'

'I can't get that sort of money in two hours—'

'Mr Dobbs can.' Number Two said, 'Ask him.'

'Ask Dobbs if he can raise a hundred thousand American dollars in two hours.'

O'Yee asked. He waited for the reply. After a moment, he nodded.

Feiffer said, 'He can get it.'

'Good.'

There was a click.

Neither of the two phones rang again.

*

Dobbs seemed to be ringing from somewhere very quiet and still. Dobbs said, 'In that case, the best thing for me to do is to send the money out by car to you at the depot.' There was a pause while he looked something up on a street map, 'The number three repair shed seems to be almost on the corner. I'll have someone bring it over in a suitcase. He said he didn't care if the serial numbers were running or not?'

'That's what he said.'

'In that case, just to confuse him, I'll make sure they're not.' Dobbs said, 'There are other ways of marking money apart from serial numbers.' He said mysteriously, 'Ultra violet, for a start.'

'Well, you've only got about ninety minutes to do it.'

Dobbs said confidently, 'You let me worry about that.' He said, 'I don't think that bugger has anything on a plane anyway.'

'I wouldn't be too certain of that if I were—'

'You just trot along in there unarmed and—'

'There wasn't any stipulation that I should be unarmed.'

'—and leave the sophisticated logic to me.' Dobbs said, 'I assume you'll have the place covered?'

'No.'

'Why not?'

'For a start, I don't have anyone to use. My other two people are out on a murder enquiry. The way Number Two was talking he's fairly confident he could lose a shadow anyway.'

'I wasn't talking about shadowing him! I meant, pick the bastard up!'

'And what does his Principal do then? We haven't the faintest idea in hell which plane the thing is on, what time it's set to go off, or even what the thing is! While you're busily questioning Number Two, Number One could be happily pressing buttons and arming switches on half the planes in Asia—'

'Balls!'

'What does that mean?'

'That means nothing's left this airport since the first incident that hasn't been torn to pieces like a hash-peddler's bloody hookah. If there's another incident planned then it's going to be carried out by a bloody Flying Saucer, because there sure as hell isn't any other way. Everything—and I mean everything —that went on board airplanes this morning was checked. Ditto for everyone—and I mean everyone.' Dobbs said, 'To show you how bloody thoroughly it was done, we caught a steward on a bloody Arab V.I.P. flight with a suppository of diamonds shoved up his arse.' He said, 'Everything that went up today in one piece is going to come down where it should in exactly the same, untouched, virginal condition.' He said, 'That bugger's bluffing. He knows it and I know it. Otherwise, why wouldn't he give a fuck about the serial numbers? He obviously knows he hasn't got the ghost of a chance of getting away with it—and I bloodywell know it too!'

'Then why kill fifty-seven people if it's all for nothing? If it's all just to—'

'You know what these Asians are like—'

'No, what are they like?'

'You know what I mean!'

'Are you saying this is all some sort of bloody *joke*?'

'It wasn't any joke to the dead passengers!'

'What the hell are you talking about?' Feiffer said, 'For Christ's sake this bugger means it!'

'Then why didn't he tell you the number of the flight?'

'Because he wants the bloody money first!'

'He knows he's never getting the money!' There was an odd tinge to Dobbs' voice. Dobbs said, 'I'm in charge of this and it's my responsibility. Once we nab him we'll find out the identity of this so-called Principal and pick him up as well.'

'And what if Number Two doesn't know the Principal's identity?'

'We'll find that out when we nab him.'

There was a silence. Feiffer said evenly, 'Keep your people out of my district unless you get prior permission from a senior officer.' He waited.

'What did you say?'

'In my estimation, the person who rang me was sufficiently

35

cocky and confident to have planned himself some sort of fool-proof escape route. If he's confident enough to have planned that, then he's also found some way of getting something on board one of your aircraft. Since the pick-up is in my district, I intend to take care of it personally. I intend to give him the money in exchange for the information. Nothing more. When I've got the information, that's the time to go hunting him, not before.' Feiffer said, 'All right?' He glanced at O'Yee.

'Was it also your estimation to tell him that I was on the other line? In your estimation, was that a clever thing to do?'

'Yes, it was! Since he apparently already knew!'

'*How* did he know?'

'He predicted it! He and his bloody Principal seem to have worked it out in advance—'

'If there is a Principal—'

'Even if there isn't—'

Dobbs said, 'There probably isn't.'

'Well, if I may make so bold, what prompts you to say that?'

'It figures there isn't, doesn't it?'

'Why does it figure there isn't?' Feiffer glanced again at O'Yee.

There was no reply.

'Dobbs—?'

Feiffer had the impression that Dobbs shrugged his shoulders and glanced around to see no one else was in the room. Dobbs said, 'He speaks Chinese, doesn't he?'

'What?'

'He speaks Chinese to you, doesn't he?'

'Hardly surprising since he is Chinese.' Feiffer looked at O'Yee curiously.

'Well then it figures, doesn't it? That there isn't a Principal.'

'I don't understand.'

There was another pause, then Dobbs said, 'Well, if there was a Principal who planned something as clever as this a second time—someone to get a second device past us while we were searching—well, he'd have to be a European, wouldn't he?' He hurried on before Feiffer could comment, 'So your Number Two would have to had learned English to talk to him about it—wouldn't he? But he doesn't speak English otherwise he would have spoken it to you.' Dobbs said, 'So there isn't any second device.'

Feiffer said, '—what?'

Dobbs said, 'All my senior officers here are Europeans. I've got a few Chinks, but they're only Junior Inspectors at best and I never let them do anything without a European along to give them orders.' He said, 'I suppose it's the same for you.' He said, 'I've been out here for over eighteen years, and you can't spend that much time in this part of the world without learning something of the basic truth about the place, can you?'

Feiffer knew what was coming. He said tonelessly, 'And what's that? The reason why Number Two couldn't have planted a second device?'

'Well, obviously—'

'Obviously—?'

Dobbs said, 'The Chinese are stupid. Without a white man to direct them they couldn't even tie their shoelaces on the right shoes.' He said, 'They're stupid.' He asked, more than a little surprised, 'You didn't know that? Someone told me you'd been in the Colony a long time—'

Feiffer said, 'I haven't been in the Colony a long time. I was born here. I live here. I intend to go on living here and unless anything dramatic happens, like my father and my grandfather before him, I'll probably die here.' He said, 'I hope that makes my position clear to you.'

There was a pause. Then Dobbs said suddenly, 'Oh—!' Something occurred to him.

'What does "oh!" mean?'

There was another pause. Dobbs said slowly, 'Oh. Father and grandfather.' He asked quietly, 'What, Daddy Wong, was it?' He asked laughing, 'Or Grandad bloody Ling Lung fucking Lee?' He said almost to himself, 'Well, now I know—' He asked happily, 'Am I right?'

There was a terrible silence.

Laughing, Dobbs hung up.

4

The two sewermen were sitting on stools at an open air food
stall on the sidewalk in Tiger Snake Road. Fortunately, at a
distance of twenty yards, the smell of food cooking was very
strong. At a distance of twenty yards, other food stalls were
crowded with people. At a distance of two yards, the food stall
at which the sewermen were sitting was deserted except for the
two sewermen. The food stall owner looked very unhappy. It
was still light but the two sewermen sat under the white glare
of a kerosene hurricane lamp hung from a corner of a food
stall by a hook. There seemed to be an aura rising from their
overalls, like heat on a desert highway. The heat aura rose up
into the lantern and then flowed out and up from it in billows
like convection currents. The people at the next food stall
twenty yards away winced every time the breeze changed. The
two sewermen went on eating. One of the people eating at the
next stall—a rotund, balding tailor with needles pinned down
the length of his working apron and a tape measure protruding
from his pocket—went 'Ugh!' and paid up. He cast a withering
look in the direction of the two sewermen and went back to his
premises. The two sewermen took no notice. They went on
munching and shovelling food into their mouths with their
chopsticks. The senior sewerman arched his back. It had been
a hard day. He went on eating. The aura kept rising.

Spencer said, 'There they are.' He and Auden manoeuvred
their way through the chewing and drinking human congestion.
There was a warm hissing sound from all the lanterns on the

stalls and a wonderful smell of pork and rice and sauces cooking on charcoal fires. The smell made Spencer feel hungry.

Auden said, 'Oh, God!' They had passed the twenty yard mark and were less than thirty feet away.

Spencer reached the two sewermen. They looked up and smiled, caught sight of Auden five yards behind and stopped smiling. Spencer said pleasantly, 'Sorry to bother you while you're eating.'

The senior sewerman said, 'That's all right.' He glanced at Auden unpleasantly.

'—we've got a few photographs we'd like you to look at if you don't mind.'

The junior sewerman looked interested. He looked at Auden. Auden tried to get downwind. There was no downwind.

'—we've sent fingerprints off to Records and we've got calls out to other Police Stations for missing persons, but we thought you might be able to offer us more immediate help.' Spencer smiled winningly. He glanced at Auden.

The sewerman said, 'Sure.' He moved. The aura turned into a billow and almost knocked Auden off his feet. Auden said with feeling, 'Oh God! ! !' He looked back to the other food stalls. People were shaking their heads in admiration or thinking that Europeans, in addition to their other failings, obviously had no sense of smell. Auden said to Spencer, 'Forget the bloody amenities and get on with it, will you!'

The senior sewerman looked at Spencer expectantly. The senior sewerman, like the junior sewerman, spoke no English. He waited for a translation from the pleasant policeman.

The pleasant policeman said in Cantonese, 'He's hoping you can help too.' (One of the other eaters, presumably doubly equipped with ears like an Alsatian dog and an ability to speak English, said, 'Oh—ha!') The pleasant policeman said, 'Here.' He handed over six Polaroid photographs, 'Have you seen any of these men before in the vicinity of—of your place of work?'

The senior sewerman looked at the photographs. At the first

picture, he stopped chewing and swallowed his mouthful of food in one gulp. At the second, he put down his chopsticks. He passed the third to his junior partner. His junior partner stopped chewing and took a swig of tea. At the fourth, the senior sewerman looked at Spencer and then at Auden. The senior sewerman glanced at the fifth and sixth photographs quickly.

Auden said, 'Look at the last two again.'

The senior sewerman looked at the last two again and passed them with the others to his partner.

Auden rubbed his nose. His nose was numb. Auden said, 'They're the bodies from your sewer.'

'The water channel.'

'Whatever.'

'The water channel. Not our sewer.' The senior sewerman said, 'The old water channel.' He said, slightly piqued, 'The old water channel is the responsibility of the Water Section of the Department of Public Works.' He said proudly—if a little weakly after the photos, 'We're the Sewer Section.' He said in a superior tone of voice, 'Not the same thing at all.'

The junior sewerman nodded. The junior sewerman asked innocently, 'Were they all hit by a tram or something?'

The senior sewerman looked at him.

Auden said, 'They were shot with a machine gun.'

The junior sewerman nodded.

Spencer said, 'Well? Have you seen any of those people in the vicinity of your manhole cover or—' Difficult to put a location on something like that without giving offence—'Have you seen them during your work?'

'Not in the sewers, no.' The junior sewerman considered re-starting his meal and then thought better of it. He said, 'The water channels are the responsibility of the Water Section crew for Hong Bay. They look after current water channels, not us.'

'The water channel wasn't a current one. It was sealed with bricks at both ends. That was why there was a hole bashed in the wall of the sewer channel to give entry to it.' Auden said,

41

'Someone took these people down through the sewer, discovered a hole knocked in a wall, led them through into a disused water channel, and bumped them off. So, have you seen any of these people—on your travels?' He glanced impatiently at the food stalls behind him. They all seemed to be deserted. Auden said, 'Well? Yes, or no?'

The senior sewerman considered something. He looked at the junior sewerman and considered something carefully. The senior sewerman said, 'Maybe.'

'What do you mean, "maybe"? Have you or bloody haven't you?' He considered for a moment running them into the cells for a quick, salutary lesson in communication. The awful possibility of that stench wafting up from the dungeons for the next two hundred years struck him all at once, and he dismissed the notion as quickly as it had come. Auden snapped, 'Well?'

The senior sewerman took up one of the photographs. It showed what happened to someone's face when it was hit by two nine millimetre high velocity jacketed bullets at five yards. The face looked like God had given it two extra eyes in the forehead and then tried to paint them out with a red paintbrush. The senior sewerman said, 'I know this one.' He took up a second photograph. In the second photograph, one of the bullets had taken all the front teeth out on its way through to the back of the throat. The senior sewerman said, 'And this one too.'

'Who are they?'

The senior sewerman hesitated.

Spencer said, 'We know that they're probably criminals and you're worried about reprisals, but—'

The senior sewerman glanced at the junior sewerman. The junior sewerman shrugged. The senior sewerman said to Spencer, 'He doesn't realise what could happen—'

Spencer said, 'I promise you, we can protect you—'

Auden said, 'Who are they?'

The senior sewerman said, 'They're the Water Section.'

'Who are?'

42

The senior sewerman said, 'Those two. They're the Water Section for Hong Kong Bay.' He said, 'Hsuang and Ching. I don't know their other names.' He said with a sigh, 'They're the two people who take care of the water channels.' The senior sewerman said quickly, 'We didn't make the hole in the wall! That was already there! We may have made a few others, but we didn't make that one!' He said, 'That one was definitely already there!'

'What were they doing in the water channel anyway?'

The senior sewerman said, 'That was their job. They were in charge of the water channels.' He said, 'We're only in charge of the sewers—'

Spencer asked, 'What holes did you make if you didn't make that one?'

'We didn't make that one! We may have made a few others in a few disused channels, but not that one!' The senior sewerman said, 'And you can tell them that too!'

'Tell who?'

'You know who!'

'Tell them what?'

'You know what!'

'No.'

The senior sewerman sighed. His face said that the game was up. He looked at his junior. His junior made a Stan Laurel face. The senior sewerman looked down into his rice. 'We make holes from our sewers into some of the old water channels that no one uses anymore—' He looked up, 'For Heaven's sake, what do you expect? We're only human!' He fixed his eyes on Auden, 'Even you, even you must be human! What would you?'

Spencer said, 'Look, I—'

Auden said, 'Are you seriously trying to tell me that you two—'

The senior sewerman said, 'Why not? No one uses them!' He looked at Spencer aggressively, 'Wouldn't you?'

Spencer said to Auden, 'Phil, I don't quite see—'

'They make holes in the walls so they can go into the old water channels for a *piss*!'

The junior sewerman said, 'We don't!'

Auden said, 'For a *shit* then!'

The junior sewerman said, 'Well . . .'

'They go into the old water channels for a shit!' Auden looked at the senior sewerman. He looked back at Spencer. He said to Spencer in English, 'They're as crazy about fucking sewers as you are!' He said to the senior sewerman in Cantonese, 'You didn't want to dirty your sewer up—right?'

The senior sewerman said, 'Right!'

'They didn't want to dirty up a fucking *sewer*!'

The senior sewerman said, '*Our* fucking sewer!'

Auden said, 'God Almighty—!'

Spencer said, 'Why didn't you tell us that in the first place? Why didn't you go into the water channel yourselves and see what the, smell was? Why just say you smelled something odd and not even investigate it?' He stopped for a moment. He said, 'You did go in, didn't you?'

The senior sewerman nodded.

'And you saw the bodies, didn't you?'

He nodded again.

Auden said, 'Then why in the name of all that's holy didn't you tell us straight away that two of the people in there were known to you? That they were bloody waterworkers?' He shouted at the senior man, 'Well? Aye?'

The senior sewerman stood up from his stool. He was very short and wizened. The senior sewerman said, 'Look at me! Where else could I get another job at my time of life?' He asked, 'Aye?' He asked, 'What else do I know except sewers?'

'So bloody what?'

The senior sewerman blinked back a tear of emotion. He said quietly, 'Well, I—' He paused, blinking. He sniffed. He looked at Spencer, at the pleasant one beseechingly.

His face began to dissolve into tears.

Spencer said, 'We won't tell a soul.'

44

The senior sewerman said, 'We've closed off all the other holes we made. All of them. We spent the whole afternoon closing them off—'

Spencer said, 'We won't tell anyone.' He said encouragingly, 'We're just very grateful you took the trouble to tell us what you—what you suspected.' He said definitely, 'You suspected something and you reported it to the police. You didn't enter the water channel to investigate because you're sewerage and the water channel is—'

The senior sewerman said, 'Thank you very much . . .'

Spencer said, 'Hsuang and Ching—right?' He wrote the names down in his notebook.

The senior sewerman nodded.

Spencer said, 'Fine. Thanks very much.' He said to Auden, in English, 'He thought the two waterworkers were down there to catch him and his friend using the old water channels for toilets.' He said in English, 'You can see that, can't you, Phil?'

'Oh, sure. I can see that. Who do they think runs the Water Section? Bloody Baby Face Nelson?' Auden said with disgust, 'Don't worry, I believe them!' He said, 'Jesus—!' He said, 'What bloody next?' He turned to go.

Spencer felt something on the sleeve of his coat. It was the junior sewerman. The junior sewerman nodded his head to the old senior sewerman. Behind his hands, the senior sewerman seemed to be crying in relief. The junior sewerman said, 'My grandfather's very grateful.' He smiled.

Spencer looked at the senior sewerman. 'Your—' to say that a family whose tradition of sewer working obviously went back generations would be interested in old Osbert and Edwin would be putting it mildly— Spencer said, enthusiastically, 'Did you know that in the nineteenth century—'

At the twenty yard mark, Auden shouted, 'Are you coming or not?'

The junior sewerman said, 'Were you going to say something?'

Spencer paused. He glanced at Auden disappearing around

the corner. He said, quickly, disappointed, 'Maybe some other time—'

He hurried through the maze of stools and stalls after Auden into Canton Street.

*

The number three repair shed in the Peking Road bus depot was cavernous. If it was built in the Victorian era, it must have been with the thought of an alternate use as a train marshalling yard in mind, or, if later, then it had been designed by an architect with his eyes firmly set on a future contract to build hangars for the Zeppelin factory. The place was enormous, dark, with high brick walls on all four sides giving way to massive steel metal roof supports and arched wrought iron arches to below them, a huge flat unpainted concrete floor that stretched the full one hundred feet to the rear wall without a single architectural undulation. A dozen or so buses in various stages of being put together or torn apart stood around in no apparent order like little plastic toys on a vast plain. Here and there were darker areas on the floor mined with unmarked grease pits for the unwary. There was a gentle hissing from an air-hose somewhere in that vast empty forest of blackness, and, somewhere else, in another oasis, the steady clicking of a battery charging machine on overnight trickle. There was not a window in the place and except for safe bulbs on power sockets in the walls and two or three mesh-covered working lamps on long electric leads left by the repair gangs on the floor and under buses, hardly any light.

Feiffer's footsteps echoed on the concrete floor. The shed was deserted for the evening meal break or between shifts. Feiffer had his coat off to show that he had left his gun outside. In that light, it would have made no difference anyway. It was cold and chill in the shed. There was the faint sound of a wind somewhere high up in the steel girders or between the bolted supports of the rusting dark wrought iron arches and

46

from time to time, a scrabble as a bird nesting somewhere up there peered down to watch him through glittering and hooded black eyes.

Feiffer flicked the aerial out on his plastic walkie talkie. There was a buzz of static as the charged air touched the cold metal of the roof. Feiffer said, 'Christopher?' He waited.

O'Yee's voice said, 'Here.'

'Where are you?'

'I've moved around to one side of the shed. I'm outside facing the corner of General Gordon Street.'

'Anyone?'

'No one who looks like our man. People coming out of tea houses and going towards restaurants and food stalls, a few kids on their way to night classes and a few bus drivers arriving for work or going home.' O'Yee said, 'I'm parked across the only side door I could see in the place. It's got a padlock on the outside.' He asked, 'Everything all right in there?'

'All right.' Feiffer went on towards one of the lights under the chassis of a dismantled bus. The clicking from the charger went on monosyllabically. 'What about the Kai Tak people?'

'After Ming delivered the suitcase to you he drove around into Yellowthread Street towards the flyover. They seem to be keeping away.' He asked, 'Have you still got the suitcase?'

Feiffer gripped the leather handles of the case. The case felt very heavy, about a hundred thousand dollars worth in small bills. 'There's not a soul in here. There are a few lights used by the repair gangs. There's one under a bus about thirty or forty feet away. I'm moving towards it. That way even if I can't see him, he'll probably see me.'

'I've got the camera out here. If he comes out this way I'll get a shot of him. Unless he tells you where the device is. In which case, I'll get him.'

'What about the uniformed people?'

'Constable Yan's across the road from the main entrance in a tea shop and Sun's further down on Generalissimo Chen Street in case our man beats it out through the car park.

47

They've both got cameras.' O'Yee said reassuringly, 'We'll get his portrait anyway.' He said, 'Just don't get shot.'

'I don't intend to.' There was a terrible *CRASH*! and he went to the floor.

'What the hell was that?'

There was a pause. Then a coughing and spluttering and then a shattering roar and then a steady beating noise from a diesel engine.

Feiffer said into the walkie talkie, 'It was an air compressor starting up. It must be on automatic.' He picked himself up from the concrete floor. 'It's like walking around in one of those old movies when a slab falls down and out comes Boris Karloff.' He said, 'It's all right now. I'm more or less in the centre of the shed as far as I can tell near a light. I think I'll just stand here and let our man find me.' There was a sudden shaft of light from the rear wall. It was a door opening. The light in the rear wall was a tiny door. A silhouette came into the light. It was bent over to get through. 'He's come in through a small door about the middle of the rear wall. It looks like some sort of delivery hatch.' The light went back to blackness, 'He's inside.' He made out a vague shadow of a tall thin man standing far away against the rear wall, 'He's here.'

The compressor cut out again on automatic and there was utter silence.

Feiffer's voice came as a hissing whisper, 'I'll leave the walkie talkie on transmit.' Feiffer said, 'He's just standing there. I don't know whether he can see me or not. He appears to be about five ten or so. I'm only getting him as a silhouette. I hope to Christ no one at Kai Tak had the bright idea of putting a bomb in this case—' He said urgently, 'He's moving. I think he's seen me. He's coming towards me fairly slowly. Appears to be looking around. Can't see a weapon. Difficult to tell.' He waited with sweat forming on his palm against the leather case handle.

A voice said in English, 'Mr Feiffer?'

Feiffer thought, "So much for Dobbs—." 'Yes.'

The voice said again, 'Mr Feiffer?'

Feiffer said, 'Here.' He took a step forward. There was the rustling sound from the birds nesting in the roof. 'Do you want me to come forward or stay here?'

There was no reply. The figure began coming towards him. 'Do you intend to tell me where the device is before or after I hand the money over to you?'

The figure stopped.

'I'm not armed. Just tell me which way you want to play it—'

The figure said in exactly the same tone as the first time, 'Mr. Feiffer?'

Feiffer said, 'Do you speak English or not?' He said in Cantonese, 'Number Two?'

The figure hesitated. The figure said, 'Um—' The figure changed its mind about something.

Feiffer said in English, 'Number Two?'

The figure said back in English, 'I am Number Two.'

'Who sent you?'

'I am Number Two.'

Feiffer said in English, 'Who told you to say that to me?'

The figure seemed to hesitate again. The figure said, 'Mr Feiffer—?' There was a rustling noise. It didn't come from the rafters. There was something behind one of the buses. Feiffer said urgently in Cantonese, 'I'm not armed. This isn't a trick—' He saw the flash of a metal badge and then another. The figure twisted. There was a snapping sound as something metal came back hard against the pressure of a case-hardened spring. The figure said, 'Aiiyaa—!' It began to run.

Feiffer saw the uniforms. He shouted at the figure in English, 'Don't run!' He thought, "It's not him!" He shouted out in Cantonese, 'No! Don't run!' There were two shots that echoed around the shed and the figure fell over.

O'Yee wrenched open the front door of the repair shed. He had his gun in his hand. There was something lying in the exact centre of the floor under a working light surrounded by Feiffer and two uniformed policemen. He walked towards them and heard Munday say, 'I'm not you, I don't shoot to kill! I shot him in both legs with nothing more lethal than birdshot!' and Feiffer saying in reply, '*I* wouldn't have shot him at all!'

O'Yee holstered his revolver. The shot man was lying on the ground holding both his knees. There seemed to be remarkably little blood.

Feiffer said, 'He was a stooge. He had nothing to do with anything. Someone told him to come in here and say "Mr Feiffer?" and "I am Number Two" and collect a suitcase.' Feiffer said to the shot man in Cantonese, 'You were told to come in here and collect a case. Right?'

The shot man shook his head.

Chief Inspector Munday said, 'He's the man all right!' He glanced at Inspector Ming. 'We'll ring Kai Tak and tell Mr Dobbs we've got him.'

Feiffer said, 'You might think to get an ambulance as well.' He looked at the shot man. The shot man was the kind of middle-aged vagrant anyone could employ to do almost anything on almost any street anywhere. He asked the shot man, 'What's your name?'

The shot man said, 'Yip.' He said, 'The man gave me twenty dollars. He told me to come here and say two things in English and then leave. He said it was a business transaction he wanted to keep quiet. He said to tell you later he was disappointed in you.'

'Later when?'

'If we talked in Cantonese.'

Feiffer said, 'Or if you were shot or arrested.'

The shot man gazed at his knees and nodded. The shot man said, 'I didn't know that.' He glanced at Munday and Ming and at the shotgun still in Munday's hand. 'I didn't know it had anything to do with the Police. He said it was just a business transaction.' The shot man said, 'I'm in big trouble, aren't I?'

'Can you stand up?'

The shot man nodded. There seemed to be tears in his eyes. He reached up and took Feiffer's hands and dragged himself to his feet. For a thin man he was heavy. He slipped against Feiffer's chest and fell back on buckled knees. He said very sadly, 'I don't know anything about police and guns!' He began crying in earnest and hid his face in his hands on the concrete floor. He said pleadingly to the floor, 'Can't you just let me go?'

'No.'

'I don't know anything about anything!' He implored Ming, 'Can't you just fix me up and let me go home?'

Inspector Ming said, 'It'll be all right.' He patted the man on the shoulder and glanced at Chief Inspector Munday on the wall telephone. He said softly to Feiffer, 'Bird shot—' He said, almost to himself, in faultless English, 'Yes, sir, bloody goddamned no, sir—' He said suddenly to Feiffer, 'Sorry, sir.'

He glanced down at the shot man.

*

At 8.10 p.m. the second aircraft ran into trouble. On a routine scheduled instruction from Kai Tak Tower, the pilot ran a complete instrument check over the Pratas Shoal, midway between Hong Kong and its destination of Taiwan. The instrument check showed that several of the hydraulics systems confirm lights seemed inoperative.

Upon further instructions from Kai Tak, the pilot aborted the flight and turned one hundred and eighty degrees back to a Hong Kong heading.

Twenty-seven minutes later, the aircraft completed its second orbit over the airport, holding to a safe circling altitude above the incoming traffic on the south runway.

Forty-five minutes later, the aircraft was ordered to land on a cleared section of the field. The Air Traffic Controller informed the pilot that it was a standard safety procedure and that crash vehicles had been alerted. The pilot ran a second check on the hydraulics and found that the lights had stopped flickering. He let out the spoilers to slow the aircraft down for its descent. The aircraft's main fuel tanks were almost empty. The pilot let down the undercarriage systems.

The undercarriage did not come down.

At 9.43 p.m., flight number 26 on the Hong Kong to Taipei short-haul run touched down on its hull and wings on south runway 6B. Even with the runway carpeted in foam, the pilot was afraid that sparks from the contact of the metal against the runway might ignite kerosene vapour in one of the empty tanks before he could use the reverse thrust of the engines to slow it down.

He closed his eyes involuntarily as the hull touched the solid runway.

In the Control Tower five hundred yards away, and in the waiting lounges of the main terminals, the sound as the vapour ignited came as a gentle *whoomph.*

The second, full detonation was devastating.

*

In the Detectives' Room at the Station, Feiffer broke the lock on the suitcase. It contained two packages wrapped up in brown paper and tied with string.

Inside each carefully wrapped package, there was a single, plain, unadorned house brick.

And absolutely nothing else.

People's ears hurt. It was as if a day-long artillery barrage had suddenly totally and utterly ceased. Their ears whistled with the silence. They put their fingers in their ears and shook them to clear the silence. There was no silence. Cars still hooted and screeched, starting up, clanked gears and revved motors, hawkers and customers shouted and cajoled, abused and vilified each other, buses still ground and hissed, pneumatic doors shut, trams rattled, doors slammed, there were bumps, bangs, baby cries, there were piledrivers working, there were still crashes, shouts, hoots, honks, scrapes, dins and drills, but there was silence.

People looked up. The sky was clear. It was morning cloudless and bright blue.

There was a stillness in the air. They looked up.

You could actually hear the bells from monasteries on the tops of hills on the outlying islands.

They looked up.

There were no aircraft in the sky.

*

Dobbs shouted down the line, 'Every seven and a quarter minutes, that's how often aircraft are supposed to take off and land at this airport! There are supposed to be thirty-one airlines picking up and delivering a thousand paying passengers an hour! Now there's nothing! Nothing's moving! Nothing!

Absolutely and utterly bloody zero!' He shouted down the line, 'I hold you responsible!'

Feiffer did not reply. Outside the Detectives' Room he could hear people arguing in the corridor and at the front desk. Someone shouted in a broad Afrikaaner accent, '*Joost tell me ploody vy!*' and then there was O'Yee's voice shouting back in his just as broad San Franciscan accent, '*Out!*' and then the voices of the Chinese Constables ordering people back into the street in Cantonese. Someone shouted something back in Japanese. O'Yee said, '*Out!*'

Dobbs said, 'What are you doing about it? You let that bastard get away, no one else! If you'd got the right bastard in the bus depot we'd have had your precious bloody Number Two rotting away in a bloody dungeon!' Dobbs said, 'I've got people out here packing the bloody corridors demanding to know when the airport's going to be opened again! Important people! People who count!'

'I've got the same thing here if it's any consolation to you.'

'It fucking isn't! The airlines want to know when I'm going to catch the person who's been getting onto their planes and killing people! The civil aircraft board have grounded everything till he's caught! They blame me!' Dobbs said, 'And I blame you!' He said suddenly ominously, 'If I ever find out that you're tied in with this in some way, what I'll do to you won't bear thinking about . . .'

'What did you get from the man Munday shot?'

'I got nothing from the man Munday shot! The man Munday shot—as you well know—was a bloody stooge! He was some stooge high on ninety percent cut opium that your Number Two or one of his cohorts picked up on the street and paid to go in and collect the money.' Dobbs said, 'Munday says you tried to warn him.'

'I tried to warn him not to run.'

'*Why* did you warn him not to run?'

'Maybe I didn't want your trigger-happy Nazis shooting

54

him. It was obvious he didn't know anything! I wanted to talk to him!'

'If he didn't know anything why did you want to talk to him?'

'Maybe I just didn't want to see the poor bugger shot dead!'

'Munday didn't happen to shoot the so-called poor bugger dead!'

'And how the hell was I supposed to know that? Munday wasn't supposed to have been there at all!'

'Lucky for you he was! Otherwise he would have gotten away completely if we'd bloodywell left it to you!'

'Gotten away with what? With a fucking *brick*?'

'Your Number Two knew we weren't going to pay him off!'

'Right! And maybe that's just the reason he sent a stooge! Maybe that's why he won't deal directly with you or anyone like you! Could that—in the wildest of all possible worlds—be remotely possible?'

'Someone told him about us, and I just wonder who it might have been . . .'

Feiffer said evenly, 'I don't get the impression from the way you behave that he would have had to have asked anybody. I would have thought your bloody personality was obvious enough to anybody at a range of two miles—'

'You keep your fucking place!'

Feiffer said, 'Just how many people were killed last night on that plane?'

'A bloody lot!'

'Then there were no survivors?'

'We lost twenty-six people! Someone put gravel in the undercarriage hydraulic box—not a lot, but just enough—all the gears were ground away when the wheels came up.' He said, 'I hope you won't take it as a personal affront, but we've already seen the people who service the box and taken their statements—'

'And?'

'And everyone's accounted for except a few Chink cleaners and messenger boys who work contract anyway.' He said, 'And for your information the poison on the first plane was cyanide.' Dobbs said, 'It's some Chinese bastard skulking around the airport on the orders of someone who knows exactly what he's doing—' Dobbs said, 'At the moment my best bet for that role is you!' He said, 'The next time your Number Two rings, I want it all tape-recorded. So far, no one's even talked to this bastard except you and from where I sit your only other contribution has been to warn some Chink stooge to watch out for my policemen!' Dobbs said, 'I don't propose to tell the authorities that the whole affair's been masterminded by some pointy-headed opium addict local, so at the moment, I'm holding off telling them that my best bet is a second-rate fucking copper from Hong Bay—but your days of grace are strictly limited.'

'Terrific.'

'It is fucking terrific! I tot up the necessaries required for this job: bloody familiarity with the locals, a knowledge of the cops posted out at Kai Tak, phone calls from someone else no one knows anything about, a strange desire to pay over the money without argument and an urge to warn criminals about the police, and I don't like the addition—'

'What about easy access to poisons and bloody hydraulics systems? Or do I have a twin brother who just happens to—'

'Listen Feiffer, I've been checking up on you. I get the impression that when it comes to fellow Europeans you're not that keen at all—'

'So I go about murdering every white man in Asia. Right?'

'That's just about the way I'm beginning to see it—'

'Odd then that my first fifty victims should be Japanese, isn't it? Or was that just an oversight on my part?'

'Don't you try to be fucking clever with me, sonny! All I want to know is just whose side you're on—!'

'I'm on the side of the victims! Or have you forgotten about them? If there was any way I could convince Number Two to

56

deal with you directly, I'd be more than delighted to pass him on! The fact is, he can't be convinced!' Feiffer said, 'I wonder why?'

'You're under surveillance, Feiffer!'

'Is that what you've told the airport people? That your chief suspect is a crooked European cop? My God, that must have impressed them? Or did you go the whole way and say I was a bloody Detective Inspector as well?'

'I told them you were a bloody Detective *Chief* Inspector!'

'You must be out of your bloody mind!'

'You just tape one of those calls, that's all! That's all you have to do—!'

'And then what?'

'And then maybe I'll believe there really might be a Number Two!'

'But that I'm still the Principal or the Boss or Number One, or whatever it is!'

'Right!'

Feiffer paused. He prompted Dobbs, 'But . . .'

'But what?'

'Oh, you know. I have to tape the call to show there really is a Number Two, *but* in order to prove for once and for all to you that I'm not the top man behind him anyway I should really—just to keep things neat—carry on and catch the top man myself—if there is one. And if there isn't, then I had better invent one. Right?'

Dobbs said, 'Right.'

'Very neat.'

'I'm glad you like it. You can take your Yankee half-caste friend O'Yee along with you to give the investigation a bit of local colour.' Dobbs said, 'Look at it this way: you'll be taking the pressure off a senior officer which is always a thoughtful thing to do, and you might even get yourself elected to the company of white men again—which is also nice—'

'Is it?'

'Oh, it is, it is.' Dobbs said, 'Try it. It'll make a nice change.'

He said, 'The tape recorder. Get one. And do it.' He said threateningly, 'And right now!'

The line from Kai Tak went dead.

*

Feiffer watched the twin spools on the tape recorder winding in Number Two's words. Number Two said, 'Naturally, I'm a little disappointed, but only in a personal sense. From a commercial point of view, the entire chain of events was totally predictable.' He said, 'I suppose I should say that I'm pleased the poor fellow wasn't shot dead in an excess of zeal, but having already disposed of quite a few people from a distance in order to protect the integrity of my commodity, I really don't give a stuff.'

'Superintendent Dobbs seems to think you don't exist. He seems to think you're a figment of my criminal imagination.'

'Oh?' Number Two said, 'Surely you're recording this conversation?'

Feiffer did not reply.

'And attempting to trace it?'

'Is there any point?' Feiffer said, 'The occasional pauses from your end are due to your glancing at a stopwatch so you'll know when to change phones.' He asked, 'Aren't they?'

Number Two made a satisfied sigh. He said happily, 'It's so nice to deal with someone who knows his business.'

'What do you want?' He glanced at O'Yee on the other line to the telephone company.

'Merely to reassure you that the unfortunate affair at the repair shed hasn't dampened my Principal's enthusiasm for the ongoing nature of the contract.' Number Two said, 'The second device—the hydraulics system on Flight 26—would have been activated whatever happened.' He asked, 'As a matter of interest, what did the Kai Tak people intend to deliver in place of the money? Cut-up newspapers?'

'Two housebricks.'

There was a pause. Evidently the hand on the stopwatch was moving towards a predetermined number. Number Two said slowly, 'Well, they won't do it again now, will they? In any event, there will of course be a penalty for non-compliance with the terms of the original agreement of fifty thousand American dollars. Instructions for delivery will reach you later.' There was a brief pause. He said suddenly, 'You really won't be able to catch us, you know. We've got the whole thing worked out much too cleverly—'

Feiffer looked over at O'Yee. O'Yee held up his hand to show he only needed a few more seconds.

Number Two said, 'Yes. . . .' He made a chuckling sound. It sounded as if he had been drinking. He said again, 'Yes . . .' He said quickly, 'You'll hear from me again.' He began chuckling. The line went dead.

Feiffer looked at O'Yee.

O'Yee replaced the telephone.

'Well?'

'Nothing.'

Feiffer's phone rang. Number Two said urgently, 'I'll only keep you a moment. I forgot to tell you: there's another device.' He said, 'No hurry about it though.' He paused for a moment. 'Tell Superintendent Dobbs to—' He changed his mind. 'No, mustn't get over-confident.' He said to himself, 'Bad mistake, over-confidence.' He said in a very business-like tone, 'You'll be informed of the procedure to follow when instructions become appropriate.'

He hung up for the second time with a sharp *click*!

*

Auden walked down the ground floor corridor of the wooden two storey building and looked under the rotten wooden staircase. He reached up and tested the frame. A section of it full of little infestation holes came away in his hand. He locked at it closely, smelled it, then tossed it onto a pile of refuse outside someone's door. Something small, nasty and multipedular scuttled away. He turned back to Dirty Elmo Fan in the corridor and said, 'Ip Kam Wing.' He glanced back down the corridor of the boarding house cum brothel cum disaster area and said, 'Well?' He walked up to Dirty Elmo Fan and looked him in the face. It was a fairly horrible, unwashed face. Auden said, 'Don't feel that the threat of a police-initiated invasion of the health and building inspector is on you, but I'd be grateful if you could help me out.' He said cheerfully to Spencer in Cantonese, 'Dirty Elmo and I are old friends.' He said, 'I don't think you know Mr Spencer, Elmo. Elmo, this is Detective Inspector Spencer. Detective Inspector Spencer is a very nice man. Bill, this is Dirty Elmo Fan, boarding house, doss house and brothel keeper extraordinary.' He said, 'Dirty Elmo isn't nice at all.' He said again to Dirty Elmo Fan, 'Ip Kam Wing.'

Dirty Elmo glanced along the corridor towards the recently inspected staircase. It looked all right to him. What could you expect for the money these days? He looked at Auden. You could expect Auden. Dirty Elmo said, 'Never heard of him.'

'No?'

Dirty Elmo shook his head. He took his cone shaped cigarette from his mouth, considered it, and then stuck it back in his mouth again. There was dirt under his fingernails so deep it looked as if it had been inserted surgically. 'You know how much I'd like to help you, Mr Auden, but I've never heard of him. Is he a bad person?'

'No, *you* are a bad person, Elmo.'

'Me, Mr Auden?' Dirty Elmo looked to Spencer to witness the unfairness of life, 'If I was a bad person—'

'You *are* a bad person, and if you don't tell me what you know about a man called Ip Kam Wing I am going to take you around to the concealment of that staircase and there I am going to methodically beat you to death.' Auden asked Spencer, 'Aren't I?'

Spencer smiled weakly. He said quickly to Elmo, 'We got the

information from Fingerprints and Criminal Records that the last known address of Ip Kam Wing was here.' Spencer said, 'He hasn't done anything wrong. We just want to find someone who knew him.' He looked at Auden.

Auden said, 'He is much nicer than me, Elmo, isn't he?'

Dirty Elmo grinned wanly.

Spencer said, 'Also known as Ip the Sniff.'

There was a moment of melodramatic silence, then, like the dawn, comprehension began to steal across the Sultan's turrets. Dirty Elmo said, 'Oooohhh, Ip the *Sniff*!'

Auden nodded again. He glanced at Spencer and winked in admiration.

Dirty Elmo said, 'Ooo-hh, *The Sniff*—!!'

Auden said in English, 'By George, I think he's got it.'

Dirty Elmo said, '*Oooohhh*, Ip the—'

Auden said, 'One more time and I'll kick your teeth in.'

Dirty Elmo Fan said, 'He's gone.'

'Gone where?'

'Gone. Gone two days, therefore: gone.' Dirty Elmo said, 'Gone two days equals gone for good. I've rented his room.'

Auden said for a second time, 'Gone where?'

'Gone. The Sniff is either here or he is gone. He sniffs about, hence: The Sniff. The Sniff sniffs out jobs for The Sniff, ergo: The Sniff has found somewhere else to work and live and has gone, result:—'

Auden said, 'One more ergo, therefore or hence and you'll be gone with him.'

'His room was vacant for two days. I rented it to someone else. This morning.'

Spencer asked, 'What did you do with his effects?'

'His what?'

Auden said, 'Did he have any bits and pieces he couldn't wear on his back or put in his pockets?'

Dirty Elmo said, 'You obviously didn't know The Sniff.'

'Who did?'

'What do you mean? *I* did.'

Auden said, 'Who came to see him?'

'No one. He was The Sniff.' Dirty Elmo Fan said, 'The Sniff was The Sniff. There are lots of people like The Sniff.' He said, 'He's gone.' He asked, 'Why? Is he coming back or something?'

Spencer said, 'He's dead.'

Dirty Elmo said, 'Uh. Well, that's life.' He asked, 'So he won't be coming back here then?'

'Not unless he can walk on water.'

Dirty Elmo said, 'The only thing The Sniff could do were odd jobs. As for walking on water—'

Spencer said, 'Mr Auden wasn't serious.'

'He knows that.' Auden said, 'What was his last job?'

'I don't know. Cleaner, messenger, odd job man. What did your records say he did?'

Spencer said, 'They say he ran an illegal street gambling game.'

'Really?' Dirty Elmo said, 'Tut, tut, tut.'

Auden said, 'And you run a brothel.'

Dirty Elmo said nothing.

Spencer said, 'Did he have any friends?'

Dirty Elmo glanced at Auden. 'No.'

'Any family?'

Dirty Elmo Fan said to Auden, 'I could say something very disparaging about your colleague's apparent innocence.'

Auden said, 'Yes, you could.' He asked, 'Do you want to?' He glanced significantly at the staircase.

Dirty Elmo said, 'To the best of my knowledge he had no friends or family. He paid for his room a week in advance, so I don't know anything about his sources of income either.'

Spencer said, 'You said he'd been away two days.'

'That's right.'

'Well, if he paid for a week in advance, then presumably he's paid up until the end of the week.'

Dirty Elmo Fan said to Auden, 'The temptation to say something is well nigh irresistible.'

Spencer said, 'Someone took him down into a sewer and shot him!'

Dirty Elmo said, 'Really? Then my action in renting his room immediately was a sound economic judgement.' He said, 'Mr Spencer, before you get much older, I should tell you that—' He looked at Auden.

Auden smiled at him. He looked at the staircase with renewed interest.

Dirty Elmo said to Spencer, 'My goodness, how terrible! Do you mean that that poor human being was cruelly murdered by the forces of crime and evil and wrenched from the fullness of life and his mother's breast in the Spring of his years? My goodness!' He said in English, for some unaccountable reason, his only word, 'Lackaday!' He said in English with a strong American accent, for a totally accountable reason, his only phrase, 'No refunds possible.'

Auden said, 'Show Mr Fan the photographs and ask him nicely if he knows any of the other victims.'

Spencer showed him the photographs. Mr Fan didn't.

Auden said to Dirty Elmo, 'How's business?'

'What business?'

Auden said, 'Whatever business it is that you do.'

'Fine, fine.' Dirty Elmo asked, 'And yourself?'

'Fine, fine.'

Dirty Elmo Fan said, 'The last time you were here to talk to me on your way to speak to Hot Time Alice Ping at The Lucky Dime, you lost control and you hit me.' He said, 'I'm glad to see now that you've given all that up.'

'It's the calming effect of Mr Spencer's presence.' He turned to go out the front door.

Dirty Elmo Fan said to Spencer, 'By the way, what a nice fair-haired boy you are. Do you know, there are people, especially sailors, who just love tall boys like you with—'

Spencer looked at him.

*

In the Detectives' Room, O'Yee took off his glasses and peered at the Sony tape recorder on Feiffer's desk. There was a long flex running from it, with a rubber plug adhering to one of the telephones. It was the sort of bugging ear that could be quickly transferred from one telephone to another. O'Yee said, 'Have you ever actually met this man Dobbs in the flesh?'

'No.' Feiffer tested the connection on the phone and flicked the tape recorder onto Record. He pressed the Pause button to hold it ready.

'I imagine him as a gigantic, red-faced bugger wearing a pair of pearl handled single action Colts in tooled leather holsters—'

'That sounds more like General Patton.'

'—or an uptight little man with a bald head and rimless spectacles.' He asked, 'Or does that sound more like General Tojo?'

'It sounds like Heinrich Himmler.' Feiffer said, 'Apart from the necessity in Dobbs' mind for me to prove that there is actually a Number Two, the theory behind the tape recorder is that some brilliant mind might actually be able to recognize what part of Asia his family originally came from.' He said, 'There was a case in Australia not so long ago with QANTAS where someone extorted a million dollars by threatening to blow up an aircraft on its way up here to Hong Kong. His voice was recorded for the benefit of the experts and they concluded unanimously that the extortionist was originally from somewhere in the very north of England or the very south of Scotland.'

'And which was it?'

Feiffer said, 'He was originally from the exact centre of London.' The phone rang and he snatched it up and hit the Record button.

*

64

On the street, Spencer said unhappily, 'I'm afraid I forgot all my police training and made my feelings about him clear. The man's an absolute and utter degenerate!' He said suddenly, 'I've got to say I'm glad you beat him up the last time you were here!' Spencer said, 'I almost—'

Auden said evenly, 'I didn't beat him up the last time I was here anymore than I beat him up this time.' He opened the car door and wound the window down, 'As a matter of fact, I've never beaten him up. As a matter of fact he's always very helpful.'

'But you said—'

'That was for the benefit of all the little ears listening at keyholes. The business about beating him up the last time on the way to The Lucky Dime was by way of telling us that The Sniff used to hang about there with that well-loved Madam, Hot Time Alice Ping. And if Elmo says it, then it's undoubtedly reliable.' He closed the car door wondering what the hell The Sniff and two waterworkers had done to end up together shot to fragments in a sewer. 'Elmo's got his business reputation to consider like everyone else.'

'But I looked at him with utter loathing! And—' Spencer said, 'He was helping us and I made him feel completely no account and rotten—'

Auden passed the car keys. He said, 'You drive.'

Spencer slapped his forehead in mortification. 'But I looked at him as if he was less than—' He said, 'How could I have been so wrong?'

Auden shook his head. He walked around to the other side of the car.

'Well, say something! Tell me whether I should go back and apologise! Tell me whether I should—'

Auden leaned on the car roof and gazed down the deserted street.

Spencer said, 'Well? What? What?' He looked back at the unwholesome entrance to Dirty Elmo's unwholesome establishment. He demanded, 'Well?'

Auden got into the car and lit a cigarette.

*

The voice at the other end of the line said, 'This is Doctor Fahy from the medical research laboratories attached to the St Paul de Chartres' hospital in Hong Bay.'

Feiffer switched off the machine. 'Yes?'

'I have got some information concerning the poison found in the stomachs of the people murdered on the aircraft yesterday. I read about it in the newspapers.'

'In that case, I suggest you ring Superintendent Dobbs at Kai Tak. He's in charge of the matter.'

'Superintendent Dobbs told me to ring you. He said you were in charge.' Doctor Fahy said, 'I have some information about the poison.' He said flatly, 'It was cyanide.'

Feiffer said, 'Yes, we know that.'

'Yes, I know you do.' Doctor Fahy said, 'However, there is one thing you don't know about it.'

'And what's that?'

Doctor Fahy said very evenly and unemotionally, 'It was ours.'

He paused for a reaction.

6

There was a plastic model of a British Chieftain tank on Gamewell's desk, lovingly painted in camouflage colours with —incongruously—full regimental and squadron markings. There was another model tank on one of his filing cabinets in Afrika Korps markings, and yet another—some sort of Russian armoured car—on a little shelf below a coloured portrait of the Queen. Also on the shelf there were various tank-like trophies denoting special or miraculous skills in handling tanks. P.A.J.S. Gamewell looked wistfully at the various tanks under the guise of considering the question. He touched at his mufti sports coat and regimental tie, glanced for a final time at the Chieftain, and said, 'Yes, we had him here at one time.' He was a very tall, bony looking young man with very long fingers. He touched his long fingers to the side of his mouth. He looked back at the row of Morgue photographs set out on his desk like a column abreast of advancing armour and said, 'His name was Lee.' He took up a manilla folder, 'I got out his file just after you rang me. His full name was Lee Wai Tak. Rank at discharge, Corporal.' He said to Auden, 'He was a rotten soldier. One of the worst I've ever run across anywhere.'

Spencer wondered what the P.A.J.S. on his desk nameplate stood for. A rank? Christian names? Spencer said politely, 'I'm sorry to have to ask, but exactly what rank are you, Mr Gamewell?'

Gamewell said, 'Captain.' He gazed briefly at one of the model tanks, 'Or Lieutenant. One or the other.' He said, 'I don't really know, as a matter of fact. Letters from the Regiment in Germany call me Captain, the Pay Office has me down as a Lieutenant, and my mother's firmly convinced that by now I should have been at least a Major.' He said pleasantly, 'Call me Patrick.' He said totally unnecessarily, 'I really haven't got too much to do with the Hong Kong forces. I'm a tank officer by trade.'

Spencer said, 'Oh.' He could see that Hong Kong, if you were a tank officer, was not the place to be. He glanced out of the barracks office window. There were a few light armoured cars in the parking area and a single self-propelled gun. But no tanks. Spencer said, 'It must be a bit disappointing for a tank man out here where there just aren't any—'

Auden said impatiently, 'Listen, Pat, the people at The Lucky Dime said—'

Lieutenant/Captain Gamewell said, 'Patrick.'

'Whatever.'

Lieutenant/Captain Gamewell said, 'Whatever is "Patrick".'

'You don't like being called Pat?'

'I don't like being called Pat.' There seemed to be a faint bugle. Gamewell said, 'I'm a reasonably friendly individual and at times I even encourage familiarity from non-commissioned officers, but the name is Patrick.' He glanced at the model of the Chieftain. It had an enormous, lethal-looking gun mounted on it. 'This man The Sniff was a friend of Lee's, was he?'

Auden said, 'Yeah.'

Gamewell looked at him.

Spencer said sweetly, 'Where is your Regiment at the moment?'

'On the Rhine.' Gamewell said, 'Right about now they're probably out on manoeuvres in the Chieftains.' He said, 'I got a letter from a friend of mine out there. The man they put into my tank when I was posted ballsed it up completely.' He said, 'He grounded the thing firmly into a ditch and it took them three days to get it out again.'

Spencer said, 'I'm sorry to hear it.'

'It's bloody nice!' Gamewell said, 'They'll have him out here next, lecturing to the local light armour.' He said happily, 'And I'll go back to the Regiment the white-haired boy.' He said with enthusiasm, 'I hope he smashes it to bits.' He glanced at the model. He said to the model, 'One thing we're not short of is tanks.' He said, 'This man Lee was one of the orderly Corporals in the office here. He started off as an armoured car driver, but he was so bloody stupid we slung him out.' He said, 'I've never heard of anyone called The Sniff.' He asked, 'Not in Tanks, was he?'

'No. He's dead.' Spencer said, 'He's the one who's been shot twice in the face in the second photo.'

Gamewell nodded. 'All I can tell you about Corporal Lee is that he was a rotten soldier and we threw him out. We were going to court martial him but fortunately he came up for re-enlistment so we were spared the trouble. Lee was a horrible slimy little man with pimples and an endless stock of excuses and dodges.' He said, 'We got rid of him.'

Auden said, 'According to our information, he was known as Bobby Lee.'

'Was he?' Gamewell said, 'He was a rotten soldier whatever he called himself.'

'Why was he chucked out?'

Gamewell considered the turret on the model tank. 'He was a thief.' He glanced at the row of Morgue photos. 'One of the other people in these photos also looks a bit familiar. I think I chucked him off the base once or twice for hanging around the food stores. Name of Hsuang or something. I made out a report about him to pass onto the M.P.s but after Lee was thrown out I didn't see him again so I just let it drop.'

Spencer said, 'His name was Hsuang. He worked in a sewer.'

'I'm hardly surprised.'

Auden said, 'Is there anything missing around here?'

'Like what?'

'Like firearms.'

Gamewell glanced at the model tank. 'Not unless someone's gone out and unscrewed a 76 millimetre gun from one of the Saladins.'

Auden said irritably, 'And has anyone?'

Gamewell said, 'Is there anything else?'

Auden said acidly, 'I was thinking of something more in the line of a sub-machine gun.'

'Only the one you already know about.'

'What one we already know about?'

Gamewell said, 'The one Lee pinched. That was why we chucked him out. We suspected him of whipping a Sterling that went missing from Stores, but we couldn't prove it so we passed it on to the M.P.s and they passed it onto the police.' He looked at Auden's face. 'Didn't they?' He said, 'It was about six or eight weeks ago.' He said quickly, 'Maybe you'd better get onto them and see if they've found it.' He said disparagingly, 'What the hell anyone would want one of those things for is beyond me.' He glanced significantly at the firepower of the Chieftain. 'We never located it and we couldn't prove that Lee actually was the one who took it. That stupid bastard probably wouldn't know which end the bullets came out anyway.' He asked suddenly, 'How was Lee killed anyway?'

Auden said, 'I'll give you two guesses.'

'Oh.' He looked at Spencer.

Spencer said, 'I had a friend in England in Tanks. The Third. By the name of Roberts.'

'Alan Roberts?'

Spencer said, 'Yes.'

'I know him!' Gamewell said, 'Very tall fella, went off to Canada at one stage to do a big wargame—'

'That's right.'

Gamewell said, 'Do you know old Alan? That's extraordinary!' He said, 'Good tank officer, Alan.' A wide smile came across his face, 'We had this awful booze-up, Alan and I, in Hamburg when we were both—'

Auden said, 'Is there anything else you can tell us about either Lee or Hsuang?'

'Not a thing.' Gamewell said, 'Spencer, is it?'

'Bill Spencer.'

Gamewell said, 'I must buy you a drink, Bill.' He said happily, 'Alan'd never forgive me if I let a friend of his go by without—' He said, 'What school did you go to, Bill?'

'The same one as Alan.'

Gamewell said, 'And me! You must have been a year or two ahead of me!' He said, 'I thought you looked vaguely familiar.' He said, 'To run across you out here—that's terrific!' He said, 'You didn't consider a career in Tanks yourself, did you?'

'I thought about the Artillery at one stage—'

Gamewell said, 'You should have come into Tanks with us! Alan'll be tickled pink to hear I ran into you—'

Auden said, 'We have to go.'

Gamewell snatched up the model of the Chieftain tank. He said enthusiastically to Spencer, 'Look. Here. Take this. I made it myself. Take this home. Bloody Artillery, you must be off your head! Here! Take it!' He glanced at Spencer and made a quick mental calculation about his age, 'Not too late yet—. So you know old Alan? Well, how about that?'

Auden said, 'We can't waste time—'

Gamewell said, 'Shut up.' He fixed his eyes happily on Spencer, 'Listen, the next time you're in England I'll take you out to our camp and let you see the Regiment in action—'

Spencer said—

Gamewell said, 'Take the tank.' He passed it over. He said happily, 'How about that?'

Spencer said, 'Well, thanks very much Mr Gamewell . . .'

'Patrick! Patrick!' He was a man whose heart moved with the tanks on the Rhine. He smiled hugely at a fellow spirit in the tankless East.

Auden said to Spencer, 'We still have to get on with catching the bugger who killed Hsuang and Lee and the rest of them, you know—'

71

Gamewell glanced at him. He smiled at Spencer. He looked back to Auden.

Gamewell said, 'What's your name again—?'

'My name is bloody *Auden*!'

'Is it?' Gamewell said, 'Well, Auden, old chap, your troubles are over.' He glanced at Spencer, 'With old Bill here on the job, how can you miss?' Gamewell said, 'Bill, you've made my day!'

Auden said, 'The Sterling sub-machine gun Lee pinched was quite probably the one someone used to kill him!'

Gamewell said intensely to Spencer, 'Have you ever seen a line of tanks going down the main streets of Berlin?' He said, 'God, Bill, what a sight!'

Auden went out and waited for Spencer in the drill square.

*

O'Yee picked up the phone. He said in English, 'Detectives. Senior Inspector—'

Number Two said, 'Where's Feiffer?' He heard a click as the tape recorder went on. He shouted, 'Turn that thing off and get me Feiffer!' He demanded, 'Why isn't he there for my call?'

O'Yee said, 'I'm afraid he's—'

'Where is he?'

'He's, um—'

Number Two said, 'Get him!'

'He's not here at the moment!'

'My Principal and I don't like being told he's not—' Number Two said, 'I'm going to ring back later. I don't talk to middle management. This is a top-level negotiation!' He paused. He said, 'You get him!'

He hung up.

*

The white tiled corridors of the medical research laboratories attached to St Paul de Chartres' Hospital gave the impression of being peopled almost entirely by intense young male and female Chinese in white coats and thick pebble-lensed glasses. There seemed to be the smell of formalin and white linen everywhere. Doctor Fahy said, 'The stuff came from Doctor Curry's laboratory. He only discovered it this morning and I got straight onto you.' He was a bald, rotund man with the authoritative manner men who had had power a long time got in their early fifties. He walked along the corridor at a pace that would have exhausted someone half his age. 'After we heard that the stuff the pathologists took from the victims' stomachs was concentrated grade cyanide, we checked our stocks.' He looked in an open door into a room where three or four white-coated people were doing something smelly to a green substance on a bench and nodded. He went on. 'Curry is one of our team doing research involving toxicology.' He said, 'Poisons. Homeopathology. The technique of neutralising the effect of one substance by introducing measured amounts of a similar substance to build up an immunity.' He said, 'It's an old field, but there's plenty of scope for new work in it, particularly in relation to certain forms of cancer.' He came to a closed glass-windowed door and pushed it open, 'Here we are.'

Feiffer went in and glanced around. There was another, stronger smell: something midway between caustic soda clearing a drain and the granulated waste from a brewery. Doctor Fahy said, 'Doctor Curry, this is Detective Chief Inspector Feiffer from the police.' He cast a quick, executive look around the laboratory to make sure all was in order, and said, 'I'll stay in the background in case there are any questions you want to ask.' He said to Curry, a short, squat man with a soft, flabby face and a sallow complexion, 'Roger, I'll just have a quick look around to see how much of this equipment you're actually using.' He looked at a Bunsen burner that had evidently not been used since Pasteur's day, 'Got to keep the costs down on unnecessary lab fittings.' He said to Feiffer, 'Just carry on without me.'

'Thank you very much.' Feiffer noticed Curry's hands. They were pitted and stained with acid. 'When did you first notice the cyanide was missing?'

'This morning. Doctor Fahy read about the business on the plane in the papers and had everyone who had poisons do a check. There was a bottle of prussic on my poisons shelf the last time I looked and today, when I checked, it wasn't there any more.' He led Feiffer to the glass-windowed door and opened it, 'You can see where the thief used a crowbar or something to break in and get it.'

'Yes.' For a vertical length of about eight inches on the door jamb, there were deep indentations where a metal instrument had been used to pry open the door. Feiffer examined the lock. There were marks on the tongue where the pressure had forced it out of its socket. 'This must have been done at least two days ago for the poison to have been used on the plane. Why is it you haven't noticed it earlier?'

'The door still works so it didn't occur to me to examine it.'

Feiffer said, 'They're very deep marks.' He looked at them more closely. 'Do you keep much in the way of poisons as a rule? Was it usual for you to have anything as powerful as prussic acid in stock?'

Curry glanced at Doctor Fahy. Fahy seemed to be carefully unscrewing a length of copper pipe attached to a bench and examining it as he went. Curry said, 'The bare absolute minimum of everything is all we're allowed to keep.' He said in a loud voice, 'And if the rarefied heights of management can find a way to cut even that down then you can bet your life they will!' He said to Fahy urgently, 'For God's sake, Frank, that's connected up for the next experiment! If you take that away I'll never be able to complete it!'

Doctor Fahy glanced at him.

Curry said in reply to a silent question, 'Yes, Frank, it does have to be a brass tube!' He said intimately to Feiffer, 'If we were doing things for the military we'd get a fortune. Since we're doing nothing more important than trying to save a few million people from disease the grants are nonexistent.' He shouted at Fahy, 'I need that flask!'

Doctor Fahy said, 'It's a specially made one. They don't come cheap, you know.'

'I know it's a specially made one! I made it myself!' Curry said to Feiffer, 'Look, all I know is what I see. The prussic's gone and there are marks on the door, conclusion: someone's broken in and taken it.' He said again in a loud voice, 'If the prussic had been worth anything, my guess would have been that it was him!'—He indicated Fahy with a corroded green finger—'The custodian of the bloody grant money!' He saw Fahy return the flask to the bench and gave a sigh of relief. 'Listen, Mr Feiffer, the situation here is that we're really hard up for money. It all goes to people perfecting new germs and bombs.' He said, 'I suppose the fingerprint people and whatnot will be along?'

'I rang them from Doctor Fahy's office.'

'The good old scientific method.' Doctor Curry said fraternally, 'Cops don't get paid that much either from what I hear. Criminals do O.K.' He said, 'Soldiers and crooks. Medicos and cops—nothing.' He said, 'It's a sad comment on something.' He said intimately, 'Do you know, if I could ever get together enough money I could go off somewhere like Switzerland and get on with my work in my own time?' He asked, 'How do you think people like Curie and Pasteur discovered things?' He said, 'On their own, with no one around counting the pennies.' He said suddenly, utilising his own brand of the scientific method, 'The Curies didn't have any pennies to count. Things are different now. You need a bloody fortune just to get the equipment.' He looked over at Doctor Fahy's creditable imitation of a technological Scrooge, 'And people like him—' He said charitably, 'Frank's actually not a bad guy. He's a good chemist in his own right. I suppose someone has to look after the financial side of things—' He said, 'You're a good copper and I'm a good researcher, so how come we get nothing out of it?'

Feiffer glanced at the marks on the door. They were very deep, amateurish. He asked casually, 'What makes you think I'm a good copper?'

'The fact that you stand around making small talk with someone like me in the vague hope you might just pick up something.'

'Is that what I'm doing?'

Curry said, 'Come on, we're both in the business of investigation. Chance discoveries favour those with a prepared mind. I wish I could tell you something else, but I can't. To be honest, I don't even care about the loss of the prussic. It wasn't anything I was using or intended to use for ages.' He said pessimistically, 'I suppose there's even the faint possibility I can get more.' He said, 'It's just a waste. I wouldn't have minded if it had been used for something sensible but just to bump a few people off on a plane is really pointless.'

Feiffer nodded.

'It's not as if the effects of prussic aren't well known.' Doctor Curry said, 'If it had been something exotic then all those deaths might have added to the bulk of scientific knowledge. As it is, there's no point in it at all.'

'I'm sure that makes the relatives of the people who were killed feel a lot better.'

'People die in their millions every year! It's nice if a few of those deaths add something to the knowledge of science in order to save future lives, otherwise it's pointless.' He said conspiratorially, 'All those doctors in the concentration camps who did experiments, they must have been torn between the desire not to kill people and the same desire to learn from the killings in order to save future generations.' He said, 'It's a problem, of course, that besets every scientist.' He said, 'It's like a policeman killing a criminal in order to save innocents.'

'The people policemen occasionally kill in the line of duty are usually fairly certainly guilty of something beforehand.'

'And the people on the plane weren't?'

'Weren't what?'

'Guilty of something?'

'Of course not.'

'Oh.' Doctor Curry said, 'I'm just trying to make my usually very boring conversation a little more interesting.' He said, 'I haven't done very well.'

'You do tend to give the impression that people are only useful as guinea pigs for saving future generations.' Feiffer said, 'When do you decide that the generation worth saving has finally arrived?'

Curry said, 'Quite right.' He said, 'You have a well-developed respect for human life.'

'And don't you?'

'Why else would I be doing medical research virtually penniless when I could be earning a fortune teaching the military how to kill people?'

'Why else?'

Curry smiled. He looked over at Doctor Fahy examining a glass distillation tube. Curry said, 'You'll have to forgive me. I tend to live in my own little world.' He saw Fahy begin to unscrew the distillation unit. He called pleadingly, 'Oh, no, Frank . . .!'

He went over to throw himself supplicating on the sacrificial altar of the Antichrist of science, Commerce.

*

O'Yee said, 'Number Two rang. He didn't sound happy. He said he'd ring back.'

'Did you record it?'

'Yep. He said he'll ring back. He didn't like talking to mere underlings so he hung up. Anything from the medical people?'

'Not much.'

'Anyone missing?'

Feiffer went to the recorder to wind it back. 'The usual contract people: cleaners and so forth—casual labour. No records. They come and go day to day.'

'Anyone with money troubles?'

'Only everybody, by the sound of it. It's a bit like the cut-price basement of Woolworth's. I got a resounding lecture on the evils of the military scientific establishment and the joys of pure research.' Feiffer pressed the Rewind button and watched the spools revolve, 'I hung around until Fingerprints and Scientific turned up and from first impressions they were less than happy. Since every corridor and room in the place is loaded with rubber gloves and overshoes to keep out infection, it's not surprising that whoever broke in had the good sense not to leave his dabs or footprints about. The amount of cyanide taken tallies almost exactly with the amount used on the plane.'

'A steal-to-contract job?'

'It looks like it.' The tape wound up and Feiffer pushed the playback button.

O'Yee said, 'This man, Number Two, strikes me as pretty unlikely to have planned the whole operation himself. For one thing, he's just a trifle too boastful to have come up with something that relies as much as it does on stealth. Do you think this Principal of his could really be some sort of businessman? I mean, apart from all this jargon Number Two uses? It's possible he's picked up a garbled version of it from listening to the Principal. What do you think?

The tape made a series of static noises from the run-in section. Feiffer said, 'It's possible.'

'You don't seem very concerned.'

Feiffer said, 'No.' He said slowly, 'I'm more concerned about what he's going to do next . . .'

On the tape, Number Two's voice began its tirade.

*

Spencer came out and joined Auden in the car. He seemed very happy. Like a birthday boy, he was clutching his tank under his arm. He got into the car and put the tank on the seat between them.

Auden said, 'O.K., so now we know that two of the bodies were sewer workers—or water workers or whatever, one of the others was The Sniff, and another was an ex-soldier named Bobby Lee. So where do we go from there?'

Spencer said, 'I'm sorry I was such a long time.'

'—and that Bobby Lee supplied the gun that killed all six of them. What else have we got to go on?'

Spencer said, 'Don't get mad because I ran across an old school chum—'

'*Chum shcumm!* Where do we bloody go from here in the serious grown-up world? Well?'

'Do you already know the answer?'

'Yes, I already bloody know the answer!'

'Where then?'

'Well, while you were chatting to your Old School Tie buddy in there, one of us, Thank God, me to be precise, got the M.P.s patched into his radio and discovered from them that Bobby Lee was employed after his discharge as a contract cleaner. One of us—even got the address of the agency that employed him. That's where we go from now.' Auden said, 'I just seem to have an aptitude for police work that you must have left behind along with your application for the jolly old Royal Artillery, aye?'

'Well, there's no need to get—'

Auden said, 'How's your bloody little toy tank? Comfy, is it?'

Spencer said, 'It's a very nice tank. He made it himself—'

'Oh, good old Chum of the Old School Tie and bunfights in the Upper Dorm—' Auden said, 'Oh, it is, it's a beautiful bloody tank—really bloody, absolutely *sooper*—!'

Spencer said, 'Oh, go jump in the bloody lake!' He took the tank up and put it on his lap protectively.

Auden looked at it. He started the car. Auden said to himself and the tank, 'Boom, bloody boom!'

They left the military compound and turned down towards the waterfront.

*

Number Two rang. He sounded angry and very malicious.

7

'My Principal is very displeased with you.' The tone was clipped.

Feiffer did not reply. The tape was running. He glanced across to O'Yee at the phone on Spencer's desk. O'Yee said softly, 'Telephone Company? Chief Engineer—trace—' He waited for a moment, then nodded. He said into the phone, 'It's me again—'

Number Two said, 'He feels you should keep yourself available for negotiations and not go running about on other matters.' He said, 'He's very angry.'

'I'm sorry to have offended him.' Feiffer said, 'Perhaps this small matter you represent is not the only affair requiring my attention—' He glanced at O'Yee. O'Yee was waiting impatiently for the trace. Feiffer said, 'I was only gone an hour.'

There was no reply.

'Are you still there?'

Number Two said suddenly viciously, 'You do what you're told, Feiffer! Don't you try to hand me a lot of double-talk! You stay in when we're calling!'

'How am I supposed to know when you're calling?'

'You just stay in, that's all!' Number Two said, 'My Principal was very angry that you missed the call. For all you know, it could have been a matter of life and death for a planeload of people!'

'Mr O'Yee was here.'

'I don't deal with subordinates! I deal with the top man!

You were chosen to be the one to negotiate and you're the one I talk to! Nobody else!' He demanded, 'Where were you?'

O'Yee said quickly into the phone, 'I don't know how much longer we can keep him on the same line . . .'

Feiffer said, 'I was out.'

'Out where?'

'None of your business.'

'Everything's my business! I said, where were you? I can find out!'

'Find out then.'

Number Two said, 'You were checking up on the sabotage. You were at one of the two places we've already used—the hydraulics place—'

'As a matter of fact, Superintendent Dobbs—'

'Then the caterers!' Number Two said, 'I'm very angry!'

'I thought you said your Principal was the one who was angry.' Feiffer looked quickly across at O'Yee. O'Yee was drumming his fingers on his desk impatiently. Feiffer said, 'I was under the impression that—'

The line went *click*!

The phone on O'Yee's desk rang. Feiffer ran out the flex on the tape-recorder and attached the microphone to the receiver.

Number Two said, 'My Principal was very displeased with you.'

O'Yee said urgently to the telephone engineer, 'He's moved lines. Here's the new number—'

Number Two said, 'You've incurred his displeasure which is a very ill-advised thing to do.'

Feiffer did not reply.

'Did you hear what I said?'

Feiffer glanced at O'Yee.

Number Two said, 'Feiffer—are you there?'

Feiffer paused a moment. He hung up.

O'Yee looked at him.

There was a pause, then the other phone on Auden's desk rang.

O'Yee said to the telephone engineer, 'Forget it. Here's the new number.' He gave the number of Auden's phone.

Auden's phone went on ringing.

O'Yee said to Feiffer, 'Well?'

Feiffer went back to his own desk and connected up the microphone to his own receiver. He waited.

The phone on Auden's desk stopped ringing.

O'Yee said to the engineer, 'Forget it . . .' He waited. He said sweetly to the engineer, 'Just hang on a moment . . .'

The phone on Feiffer's desk rang and he picked it up.

O'Yee gave the tracing engineer the new number.

Number Two shrieked down the line, '*What the hell do you think you're playing at?*'

Feiffer did not reply.

'The Principal won't like this! You cross him and you'll—'

Feiffer said evenly, 'I listened to the tape of your earlier conversation with Mr O'Yee. You sounded near hysterical. Since at that time your so-called Principal had no idea whether I was in or out, I have to assume you were near hysterical on your own account.' He said pleasantly, 'Hysteria is the stuff of office-boys, not business executives. Regretfully, I begin to have the feeling that you may not be the person to deal with at all. Your earlier loss of control and this outburst at the moment tend to cause me to believe that you're not sufficiently commercially responsible or objective enough to deal with.' He said, 'To be honest, I don't suppose you even know if there's anything on at the moment or not.'

Number Two said vehemently, 'Just who do you think arranged everything? Just who do you think got everyone organised so the devices would work? Just who do you think is in charge of everything on the real day-to-day basis?'

'The Principal?'

Number Two said, 'Me!'

'Then why get so angry if your little telephone call has to be delivered to a subordinate? After all, you're only a subordinate yourself.'

I'm a *partner*!'

'Oh?'

Number Two said, 'I know what you're trying to do—you're trying to bait me so I'll stay on the line so your little Eurasian mate can get a trace in. I've got a stopwatch on the conversation. He's got thirty seconds left.'

O'Yee held up five fingers seven times. The engineer only needed a little over half a minute.

Feiffer said, 'My little Eurasian mate, as you call him, makes it fifty seconds.' He asked, 'Well, what do you want to say?'

Number Two said, 'My Principal knows you! He warned me about this! He said you liked playing little games with conceited people!' He said, 'I'm not conceited! I don't like listening to the sound of my own voice, so you can forget it!' He said, 'Twenty seconds.'

'Your Principal knows me?'

'He knows you all right!'

'Knows about me, you mean. All your careful market research.'

'Closer than that! He knows everything about you!'

'So he says.'

'If he says it, he does!'

'He's a criminal, is he? Someone I've arrested before?'

Number Two said, 'Fifteen seconds.'

O'Yee whispered pleadingly down the line, 'Hurry . . .'

'He's respectable then? A businessman?'

Number Two did not reply.

'And he's got another device all set up that you don't even know about. Right?'

'Ten seconds.' Number Two said suddenly calmly, 'The fact that there's a non-participatory backer in this transaction is no reflection on my own abilities to deal with the day-to-day situation as it arises.' He said to himself, 'No, no reflection at all . . .'

Feiffer said, 'Ten seconds.'

84

There was a pause. He thought he heard Number Two make a sudden chuckling noise.

Feiffer said, 'Nine.' He looked at O'Yee.

Number Two said, 'Three, as a matter of fact.' He said evenly, 'I'll be back in touch.' He said, 'Nice try.' He paused. Feiffer watched the second hand on the wall clock.

Feiffer said—

O'Yee said, 'Five seconds and we've got him!'

Feiffer said, 'Listen—'

The line went dead.

O'Yee hung up his phone. He shook his head in disgust. The phone on his own desk rang and he picked it up and snapped, 'O'Yee.'

Number Two said, 'Quick, get Feiffer!' He said as soon as Feiffer came on the line, 'Listen, you, don't you ever try to get clever with me again! I know you've got the tape recorder on the other phone and you don't try to catch me out so easily! All right?' He snarled down the line, 'You get some respect for me damn quick or there'll be so many bodies around you'll have to wear water-wings to swim through the blood!' He said, 'Just to fix the point in your mind that I've got it all over you, I'm going to ring back on your phone in three seconds and make a few things clear about power and relationships.' He said, 'So plug your recorder in damn quick and maybe I'll even give you a clue.' He hung up.

O'Yee said, 'What did—' Feiffer's phone rang. He snapped the tape recorder on to Record.

Feiffer said, 'Yes?'

There was a pause, then Number Two said very softly and intimately, 'Harry? There's nobody else round, is there?' He paused. 'Harry, I'm really glad you're in on this with us. You've no idea how much easier it is having an inside man.' He said, 'That was a nice exchange we just recorded.' He said, 'Tell me, what do you think Dobbs will make of it?' He said cheerfully, 'Think of your thirty per cent split—you should worry!' He said happily, 'Cheers . . .'

The conversation, every word of which had gone turning carefully into the tape recorder, was terminated with a gentle—
click.

*

O'Yee said, 'You must be kidding! Of course you're going to bloodywell erase it.'

'If bloody Number Two's market research is so damn good, then he would have known I *wouldn't* erase it. He knows I'm not involved in it and I know I'm not involved in it. So why bother?'

'Because bloody *Dobbs* doesn't know you're not involved in it!'

Feiffer said, 'If he's done his market research the way he claims he'll know my reaction to something like this is to leave it on the assumption that, sooner or later, it might just fit in somewhere—'

O'Yee said, 'Sure! Like in the Chateau d'If or in the New York Tombs!'

Feiffer said, 'I'll leave it in and Dobbs can make what he will of it.' He said slowly, 'Number Two had a point about one thing: a man on the inside would be very helpful indeed.' He said significantly, 'I'll be interested to see what the next move is from Kai Tak.'

'If you're still at bloody large to see it!' O'Yee said, 'You don't really think Dobbs has anything to do with it?'

'Dobbs certainly seems to think *I* have.'

'Dobbs is a bloody Superintendent! You don't honestly think he's capable of killing almost a hundred people!'

'Someone is.'

'But Dobbs—' O'Yee said, 'It isn't possible—is it?' He said, 'He thinks it's *you!*'

Feiffer said, 'Maybe it is.'

'Oh, come on!'

'Have we got another clean spool of recording tape?'

'In the cupboard.'

'Get it, would you, Christopher? And wind it on in case Number Two decides to ring again.'

'And what about the old tape? What are you going to do about that?'

'I told you. I'm going to send it around to Dobbs.'

'Uncut?'

'Uncut.' Feiffer said, 'We'll just see what he makes of it all.' He sounded very interested. He paused, thinking about something.

O'Yee said, 'Words fail me.' He went to the cupboard to get the new tape.

*

The East Wind Cleaners and Messengers Employment Agency was in Hong Bay Beach Road, not far from the bus depot, on the top floor of a kapok and duck feathers warehouse. (For pillows and mattresses.) The smell from the stacked fresh materials downstairs came up the rickety stairs to the fourth floor office of the agency like a poisonous cloud of pollen at the height of the sinusitis season. Spencer blew his nose on a linen handkerchief. The linen made him sneeze. He went into the outer office of the agency behind Auden and shut the door. He sneezed again.

The male receptionist at the unpainted pine desk was an emaciated middle-aged Chinese wearing an open-necked white shirt. He had hollow cheeks, like an opium smoker.

Spencer sneezed.

The receptionist said, 'Well?'

Spencer got out his warrant card and thrust it under the receptionist's nose. The receptionist sneezed.

There was an orgy of sneezing.

Spencer gasped out, 'The boss—the man in charge—'

The receptionist sneezed. He jerked his thumb to a door.

Auden said, 'In there?' He sneezed.

The receptionist nodded. 'Yes—(sneeze)—yes!'

Auden and Spencer made it to the door and pushed it open. There was another door just inside, like an airlock. Auden pushed the second door open.

Spencer sneezed.

Auden—

The room was air-conditioned, fresh and ozone-rich. They stopped sneezing. Spencer said in English, 'Thank God!' He looked at the man behind the desk in the carpeted room. Spencer said in Cantonese, 'Police. We're sorry to bother you, but—'

Auden said, 'Mr—?'

'Wu.' The man stood up and came forward to shake their hands. He was a slight Chinese in his early thirties wearing a tight, well-pressed suit and a striped shirt. The collars on the shirt were buttoned-down. He had a very firm handshake. He went back to his desk and waved to the two chairs facing it. There was a very expensive Rolex watch on his wrist that looked as if it showed the time in three places on Earth simultaneously and threw in the phases of the Moon and the equinoxes of Saturn for good measure. P. K. Wu said in English with a soft Boston accent, 'P. K. Wu, to be precise. How can I help you?' He said before either of them had time to answer, 'Forgive the humble appearance of my office.' He said quickly, 'Even Henry Ford started off in a dirty garage.'

Spencer said, 'Did he?'

P.K. Wu said, 'Yes.'

Auden laid out the six photographs on the desk. He asked, 'Do you know any of these people?'

'They look dead.'

'They are dead. Do you know any of them?'

P.K. Wu said, 'You're from Yellowthread Street Station or—?'

'Yellowthread Street.'

P.K. Wu said, 'If they're dead, what you mean is, *did* I know any of these people?'

'*Did* you know any of these people?'

'No.' P.K. Wu pushed the photographs back to Auden.

Auden said, 'At least one of them was employed by you.'

'Oh? Which one?'

'That's what I want you to tell us.'

P.K. Wu said, 'I don't remember faces. I remember names, figures, dates, percentages and currency conversion tables. I keep my mind uncluttered for the battle of commerce. If you know the names then I'll remember them.'

Auden said, 'Bobby Lee.'

'Yes—'

Auden said, 'The Sniff.'

'The what?'

'Otherwise known as Ip Kam Wing.'

'Yes—'

'You know him?' He said quickly, 'You knew him?'

'I knew both of them.'

'We're trying to find out where they worked and who their friends were—'

P.K. Wu said, 'At one time, they both worked for me.' He said, 'The one you call The Sniff—Ip Kam Wing—was a convicted criminal.'

'We know that.'

P.K. Wu said, 'I'd like at this point to say that I'm the kind of man who gave people who'd made one little mistake in life a second chance, but I'm not. The fact is, he worked cheap.'

'Worked as what?'

'As a cleaner.' P.K. Wu said, 'That's the sort of business I'm in. I run an agency that supplies casual cleaners and messengers.' He said, 'The other one, Lee, worked as a messenger.'

Spencer said, 'The other two were employed by the Waterworks. Hsuang and Ching.'

P.K. Wu shrugged. He shook his head.

Auden said, 'Where was Bobby Lee last employed? Do you have a file index?'

P.K. Wu tapped his temple. 'Lee was employed by a firm over in Tiger Snake Road.' He gave Auden the number. 'And Ip by another firm to do with light industry.' He gave them that address as well. 'Ip was a cleaner and Lee worked as a messenger. They both worked for about two weeks and then moved on. I got my commission so I couldn't care less.' He said, 'There are plenty of people around who need a few weeks work and plenty of people who want them. I bring them together for a fee.' There was a sudden buzzing as the alarm on the elaborate watch on his wrist went off. 'Anything else?'

Spencer said, 'Is there anyone else on your books who's missing?'

'This is the casual labour market, not the Deutsches Volkswagen Werk.' Wu said, 'They come and go, go and come.' He said, 'My receptionist'll be gone this time next week. At one time or another everybody is missing.'

Spencer said, 'Your receptionist looks like an opium addict.'

'He is.' P.K. Wu said, 'But like everyone else he's got a wife and children and grandparents and someone had to give him a second chance in life—'

Spencer said, 'Oh.' He looked at Auden.

P.K. Wu said, 'And he works cheap.' He smiled blandly, the smile of a man on his way to the top.

*

Dobbs' voice said down the line, 'Well? What do you want?'

Feiffer said, 'I went round to the Medical people on your direction and talked to the man in charge and one of his chemists. The poison came from one of their labs. There were jimmy marks on the door where someone used a crowbar to spring the lock. A fairly neat job with hardly any damage done and no fingerprints.' He said, 'The same as the hydraulic people?'

'The hydraulics job was done from the inside, or someone just climbed in through a window.' Dobbs said patronisingly, 'There's not a great need for security in a bloody grease-pit compared to a place chockful of bloody poison.' He asked, 'What about the caterers? Your report says that was done from the inside as well.'

'Right.'

Dobbs said, 'You may be interested to know that we're beginning to get aircraft back into the air here.'

'I thought you sounded slightly less put-upon.'

'Oh, I'm still put-upon, but at least we've got aircraft up in the air again.' Dobbs' voice sounded very cold and controlled, 'I suppose it must come as just a tiny bit of a disappointment to you.'

'Why should it?'

Dobbs said, 'So far, reviewing the evidence, I haven't got much to go on, but when an old dog like me gets an itch on his arse and that itch's name is bloody Feiffer, I start to go around ringing any other old dogs I know and asking them if they've ever had the same itch.' Dobbs said, 'I've got an application in to search your apartment and view your bank statements.'

There was silence.

'So your fucking days out of jail are strictly limited, Feiffer!'

'Maybe someone else's are as well—'

'What does that mean—if anything?'

Feiffer said, 'I've sent the latest tape around to you by messenger. It should have arrived by now.'

'And?'

'Have you played it yet?'

'When I get it, I will!' Dobbs said, 'Why? What's on it?'

'Nothing.'

'What do you mean, "nothing"?' Dobbs said, 'If it should have arrived by now, I'll go out and find it and put it on—what do you mean, "nothing"?'

Feiffer said, 'I have to go.'

'Well? What does "nothing" in that tone of voice mean? What the hell's on it?' Dobbs said, 'I'll find it right bloody now! You bank on it!'

Feiffer hung up.

O'Yee was out in the corridor, and, except for the steady ticking of the wall clock, the Detectives' Room was sepulchrally silent.

8

In the Detectives' Room, Feiffer motioned for O'Yee to pick up the extension to his phone. Auden's voice was on the line. Auden said, '—we just thought it was an odd coincidence, but after the second time it struck us a little too hot to be coincidental.' He said, 'And sure enough, it was the exact right section to have been working in—'

O'Yee said, 'Phil, Christopher O'Yee. I've got the extension. Do you mind going through it again?' He glanced at Feiffer. Feiffer was thumbing over pages in his notebook looking for something. He nodded. 'It's O.K. with Harry.'

'The six bodies we found in the water channel. Two of them were actual sewer cum water workers who had something resembling a right to be there, the others apparently didn't. We identified one of the others as a man called Ip Kam Wing: a smalltime crook and sometime casual labourer, and another as an ex-soldier named Bobby Lee. Lee, it turns out, was kicked out of the Army for allegedly ripping off a sub-machine gun. The people in the channel were all killed with a sub-machine gun.' Auden said, 'Well, so far, so good. It turns out that both Ip and Lee worked at one time for a gang called the East Wind Cleaners and Messengers Employment Agency, run by a character called P.K. Wu. Wu, after a bit of pushing, remembered that Lee had been employed as a messenger in Tiger Snake Road by a firm catering flight meals for aircraft.' He paused to wait for O'Yee's reaction. There was none. 'And Ip, surprise, surprise, worked in the place where hydraulic units for aircraft are serviced at Kai Tak—in the exact section.'

'What about the other two bodies?'

'I think we've done well enough on the first four!'

'So you've got nothing on the other two yet?'

Auden said, 'So, as I was just telling Harry, being good little co-operative coppers, Spencer and I immediately hot-footed it over to Kai Tak to tell them what we knew. What we knew couldn't have interested them less. Some brass-buttoned Chief Inspector named Munday. Munday says the matter is well in hand and that assistance from Yellowthread Street is not appreciated. Munday further quietly advises Spencer and me to put in for a quick transfer before all is too late. What he means by that only he knows.' Auden said, 'Munday then makes a series of mysterious noises and asks me what I think my promotion chances are over here and how much does Chief Inspector Feiffer have in the bank, do I know?' Auden said, 'Christopher, would somebody mind telling me just what's supposed to be going on?' He said, miffed, 'I thought we'd done a bloody good piece of detective work. I didn't expect the instant granting of a bloody Golden Dagger Award for it, but at least—'

O'Yee said, 'Kai Tak think they already know who's behind the airline business.'

'Yeah, these two, Ip and Lee, for a bloody start!'

'The man behind those two.'

'Then why the hell don't they tell us?'

'They probably think you already know.'

'Well, I bloody don't! What are we supposed to do now? If it's their case they should have taken our information and followed it up. And what's all this jazz about promotion prospects and how much loot Feiffer's got in the bloody bank?' He asked suddenly, 'Is he still on the other line?'

Feiffer said, 'I'm still here.'

'Well, what's it about?'

'That depends on what you told them.'

'I didn't tell them anything! They wouldn't let me tell them

94

anything! They just about chucked us physically out of the office there! How the hell do I know how much you've got salted away in Swiss banks?' He said, 'I didn't even know until they told me that you had a Swiss bank!'

'I haven't.'

'Well that bloody proves it then, doesn't it?' Auden said beseechingly, 'Listen, I know Spencer and I, as the mere underlings of this outfit, don't count for more than a spit on the bloody sidewalk, but would someone mind telling us just what's going on?'

Feiffer said, 'Have you got any leads to follow with the other two bodies?'

'No, we haven't got any leads to follow with the other two bodies!'

'What about this employment agency? This man Wu?'

'Wu employs people who work cheap. He can't remember one from the other unless he's got the names written out in large letters under his nose. Since we don't have the names he doesn't have the information.'

'Have you checked the medical lab at St Paul's?'

'We went straight around there after the story about Lee working for the caterers. We saw a bloke named Fahy and showed him the pictures of the victims. None of them had ever worked there. We checked with the Head Cleaner—' He said dismally, 'At the time, I actually thought there was a joke in there since the place doubles as a dissecting lab. Now I'm not so sure—and the Head Cleaner made it clear that none of the dead men had ever worked there or had anything to do with anything. Apparently, you have to be vetted if you're going to work in a hospital, so since the lab was broken into anyway by someone outside, we didn't pursue it.' He said, 'Isn't anyone going to have the common decency to put us out of our misery and tell us what's going on?' There was no reply. Auden said to someone, or to himself, 'Nope, no one is.' He said desperately, 'With the last vestige of my copperly enthusiasm I ask someone to tell me at least who I give the information to if

95

nobody wants it—' He said again to the someone, 'Nobody wants to know.' He said desperately, 'Who the hell's handling this airline business anyhow?'

O'Yee said, 'We are.'

'*We* are?'

'Right.'

'What the hell has it got to do with us?'

'As you said, the Golden Dagger goes to the best detectives.'

'What the blue blazes does that mean? How can we handle it? We're miles from the airport, how the hell can it be our case? The bodies were obviously just dumped in our lap to throw suspicion off and to get rid of the damn things. Now we've established that there's some sort of connection, it's up to Kai Tak to take it over with a few well-chosen words of thanks.' He asked O'Yee, 'Isn't it?' There was a click on the line. 'Harry—?'

O'Yee said, 'I'm still here.'

Auden dropped his voice, 'Has he hung up?'

'Yes.'

Auden said, 'What the hell's going on, Christopher? What's all this jazz about Feiffer? That guy Munday actually asked, in our considered opinion, just how desperate he was for money and did his bitch of a wife have expensive tastes?'

'And?'

Auden said, 'Spencer asked him in turn whether or not his bitch of a wife would be happy having him home tonight without any teeth.'

'You're joking—'

'Am I?' Auden said, 'And another thing, who's this man Dobbs they keep talking about out there? He sounds like the cop next to God. Who is he anyway?'

O'Yee glanced at Feiffer. Feiffer was making notes in his book and flipping back through the pages looking for correlations. O'Yee said quietly, 'Superintendent Dobbs is in charge of Kai Tak security.'

'Hasn't done much of a job so far, has he?'

'Spencer didn't say that too, did he?'

'No, I did.' Auden said, 'It was at that stage that the chuckers-out were called in.' Auden said, 'Christopher, you must admit, leaving aside my many and oft-quoted failings for a moment, that, at heart, I'm not such a bad guy ... .'

O'Yee did not reply.

'Well, at least admit you've met worse!'

'I've met worse.'

'Then would you mind telling me what's going on?'

'Sorry. No.'

'Oh, great! What are we supposed to do now?'

'You'd better keep asking around for the two other bodies in case—'

'Ask who? Who are we supposed to ask? We've come to a dead end. It should go on to Kai Tak. Who do we ask?'

'Did you show the photos around the airport?'

'Show them around at Kai Tak! Are you putting me on?'

'Try the various cleaning departments first and, say, the services people—'

'Why don't I just find a quiet spot out there and we can walk directly into a couple of propellers?'

'They have jets these days.'

'Oh, even better! Straight up the fucking—'

'—then go back to the hydraulics and catering people and see if they know anyone who knew either of the dead men who worked for them.'

'We've already done that!' Auden said, 'Are you trying to keep us away from the Station? Is that it?'

O'Yee did not reply.

'What the hell's going on down there?'

O'Yee said, 'Look, just do the best you can, would you?'

'What do you mean, just do the best you can? We've done the best we can and it turned out to be pretty good! We thought it was pretty good anyway!' Auden said, 'Listen, Christopher, pardon me for being so bloody thick, but—'

O'Yee said, 'I'll leave it to you.'

'What about the work we've already done?'

O'Yee gritted his teeth.

Auden said, 'Well?'

O'Yee said, 'Try to find out who the other two dead men were.'

'And then what?'

'And then tell us.'

'*Why*?'

'And if you can find out, where they worked.' O'Yee said, 'I have the horrible feeling we'll be hearing about it ourselves soon enough, but if you and Spencer can get there first—'

'Get where first?' Auden said, 'This is insane!'

O'Yee said, 'We appreciate it.'

'Who is *we*?' Auden said, 'Give me bloody strength!'

O'Yee glanced at Feiffer. There was a brief silence from Auden's end of the line. O'Yee hung up softly. He said to Feiffer, 'Spencer threatened to take out a few of Munday's teeth.' He looked over. Feiffer's eyes stayed on the notebook. O'Yee glanced around the room. He tried to think of something to say. He took out a cigarette from the pack on his desk and lit it. It was a new brand his wife had bought him to help cut down. He drew in on it.

It tasted like hell.

*

On the phone, the Commander's voice sounded very cold and angry. The Commander said, 'Listen, Harry, not to mince words, I've just had Superintendent Dobbs from Kai Tak in my office. He wants my permission to apply to Internal Affairs for an investigating order on you. He wants you suspended from the Force while his people and the soft-heeled mob from Internal Affairs take you to pieces. I assume you know why.'

'Yes, sir.'

'Well?'

'Well what?'

'Well, what's the truth behind it? Dobbs told me some cock-and-bull story that you're in the process of masterminding this business with the airlines and that you actively and openly attempted to sabotage the arrest of one of the people involved in it. Is that true?'

'Do you think it's true?'

'It doesn't happen to matter what I think! I've been handed an official request for an internal investigation by a senior officer and I want to know what's behind it!'

'There's nothing behind it.'

'He tells me you've been sending your people around to Kai Tak with phoney stories about bodies in sewers to throw him off, and that he's got hard evidence to back up his contention that you're involved up to your ears. He played me a tape recording purporting to be from this man, Number Two, in which he actually thanks you for your help and talks about your share of the extortion money—'

'And did he tell you where the tape came from?'

'I know where the tape came from! It came from you. And I know that no one in his right mind would have left it on if any part of it was true. However, Dobbs is firmly convinced that it's all part of your plan and that you left it on—in fact, encouraged Number Two to record it—just to make his case look weak. That's more than a little lunatic, I know, but that's how he views it, and you must admit that to someone who doesn't know you, it doesn't look good.' The Commander said suddenly, 'Even to your most bosom buddy it'd look nothing less than fucking incriminating!' He demanded, 'So what's behind it?'

'What's behind it is that Dobbs has it in his head that it's all my fault. Dobbs is taking a lot of flak from the Kai Tak people and if he can mutter darkly about crooked coppers it adds a little more mitigation to his own bloody inefficiency.' Feiffer said, 'If you want my considered guess as to the identity of the bloody Principal—if there is one—then you could do worse than look at Mr bloody Dobbs himself.'

'Are you serious?'

'Was he?'

The Commander said, 'You just explained to me why Dobbs is out to get you and why he's a bloody lunatic for doing it, and now you tell me you yourself are out to get Dobbs—'

'I told you it was nothing more than my considered guess.'

'His considered guess is you!' The Commander said, 'Who's in charge of this case anyway?'

'Dobbs seems to think I am. It suits him to push it off onto someone else.'

'Taking the line that if he gives you enough rope, you'll—?'

'Right.'

The Commander said, 'Does this individual, Number Two, ever contact anyone else?'

'Not so far.'

'Just you.'

'Just me.'

There was a pause. 'Then you had better clear it up, Harry, and pretty damn quick too.'

'So it's my case?'

'Would you rather it was Dobbs'?'

'No, I wouldn't, as a matter of fact!'

'O.K., then it's yours. I've told Dobbs I'll give his accusation against you consideration. I'll give your accusation against him the same. Fair enough?'

'Agreed.'

The Commander said, 'I don't like it, Harry, not one bit.'

'No, sir.'

'Is there anything you want to tell me?'

'No!'

'Then bloodywell get it cleared up!' There was a sharp click as the Commander rammed the receiver violently down on its cradle.

Feiffer glanced at O'Yee. O'Yee's phone rang and he picked it up.

Feiffer thought that what everybody seemed to have forgotten was that there were over eighty people dead. O'Yee stood up and brought the phone over to his desk. He handed it to Feiffer wordlessly.

Number Two's voice said, 'Ah. Events have prompted me to add a trifle more despatch to our schedule . . .' He said, 'Now listen carefully—'

*

Dobbs sounded as if he was speaking from the telephone in the silent room again. Feiffer said, 'Number Two says he wants one hundred and fifty thousand American dollars.'

'The price has gone up, has it?'

'That's what he said.'

'Did he also say where he wanted to pick it up? Or shall I just have a cheque drawn in your favour to a numbered Swiss account and drop it in the post?'

'He said the money was to be delivered to me here at Yellowthread Street by one of your policemen. He said it was to be here ready for delivery to him later today.'

'When?'

'He didn't say.'

'Didn't he?'

'No.'

Dobbs said, 'Yes, he did. Or, of course, he didn't have to, did he?'

'Are you going to supply the money or not?'

'Why should we?'

'Because he says that if you don't, you'll get another surprise on one of your little airplanes.' Feiffer said before Dobbs could comment, 'I quote him exactly.' He said wearily, 'It's on tape.'

'Which, no doubt, you'll be having one of your little subordinate liars hurry around to me together with more cock about bodies in sewers—'

'Which I shall not be sending on to you.'

'Oh?' Dobbs sounded amused.

'The tapes will be kept at this Station as evidence.'

'Evidence?' Dobbs made a chuckling sound, 'Against whom?'

'Do you propose to get the money or not?'

'Which denominations do you prefer?'

'He didn't stipulate.'

'I know he didn't. He probably didn't even ring. I'm asking you which denominations *you* prefer.' Dobbs said, 'You may as well enjoy it while you can.'

'He didn't stipulate particular denominations so I therefore presume the choice is entirely up to you.'

There was a pause. Dobbs said, 'A word of advice at this stage, by the way, would be for you to warn your junior detectives not to go around threatening senior uniformed officers—'

'Do you propose to comply with Number Two's directions, or not?'

'Did you hear what I said?'

Nothing.

Dobbs said, 'The so-called detective in question was someone called Spencer. He was asked a civil question by Chief Inspector Munday, whereupon he threatened Mr Munday with violence.'

Feiffer waited.

Dobbs said, 'Mr Spencer is going to find himself before a disciplinary hearing when this is all over.'

'Yes or no?'

Dobbs said, 'Don't try to ignore me, Feiffer.' His voice sounded very calm and confident.

'The impression I gained from my conversation with Number Two was that the device was set for sometime later today. It might be an idea to ground aircraft for the next twenty-four hours until searches can be—'

Dobbs said, 'The threat to Mr Munday was made in the presence of Inspector Ming and two uniformed Constables.'

'One hundred and fifty thousand dollars. Yes, or no?'

Dobbs shouted, 'Did you hear what I said?'

'Yes! I heard what you said! And I bloodywell heard what Munday said, and Munday can count himself lucky I wasn't there or he'd have had to have had his brass buttons removed from his bloody tunic by fucking open-heart surgery!'

'I'm writing all this down.'

'You do that!'

'So just where do you claim this device is supposed to be planted?'

'I don't claim it's planted anywhere! That's your job! Mine is to be the bloody delivery boy! The money, yes or no?'

'When do you want it!'

'Now!'

'I'll send Inspector Ming around with it.'

'You do that!'

Dobbs said, 'Interesting, isn't it, the way the mention of your wife seems to get everyone around you going?' He said, 'The way your man Spencer came to her defence, if I was the sort of cop with a dirty mind, I'd just have to assume that—'

Feiffer felt his hand go clammy on the receiver.

'Still, I suppose one way to win friends and influence people—' He asked, 'Do you want to make any comment for the record?'

Feiffer's knuckles were white on the telephone. He drew a long breath.

'No? No comment?'

Feiffer said, 'I'll be here when Ming comes.'

Dobbs began laughing.

Feiffer said, 'What you seem to have totally forgotten is that there are over eighty people dead!'

'What's her name? Nicola, isn't it? White woman is she? Interesting that.' He said, 'I must ask your man Spencer about it.' He said in execrable French, '*Cherchez la femme*—isn't that right?' He asked, 'Touched a nerve, have I?' He said, 'Yes, I believe I have.'

He burst into a peal of laughter a moment before the connection to the silent room went dead.

Inspector Ming glanced at the Eurasian, O'Yee, and then a
the open suitcase on Feiffer's desk. The suitcase contained
hundred and fifty thousand American dollars in ten and twent
dollar bills, a total of ten thousand notes, held together in thic
wads by rubber bands. The suitcase was a deep one, but th
notes came to above the top of it. Ming said, 'It's all there,
and glanced at O'Yee for the second time in as many moments
He asked, 'Is there anything else?'

O'Yee shook his head.

Inspector Ming looked at Feiffer's hands on th
suitcase as he closed it and snapped the locks. They wer
shaking.

Inspector Ming glanced again at O'Yee.

The noise from a 707 warming up in one of the engine tes
hangars was deafening. Auden shouted to Spencer, 'Shov
him!' He took the Ground Crew Chief by the shoulder and
shouted in his ear, 'Do you know any of these people?'

. The Ground Crew Chief shouted back, 'What?'

'These people!' Auden pushed the Ground Crew Chief i
the direction of the sheaf of photographs in Spencer's hand
'Do you know any of them?'

'No!' The 707 ran up a few decibels higher and drowne
out everything. The Ground Crew Chief shrieked back, 'As
him!!' He pointed at something.

'Who?'

'Him!!' The Ground Crew Chief stretched a greasy finge
towards the corner of the hangar where there was someon
coming. He shouted above the din, 'That's Chief Inspecto
Munday! Ask him—!'

He was suddenly alarmed by the fact that, at the sight of

policeman coming to see if he could help them, two other policemen should start running away like hell.

*

Number Two had directed him to wait on the steps of the Police Station, alone, looking across Yellowthread Street in the direction of the Singapore-China-Tokyo Bank. The suitcase felt very heavy in his hand. He changed it over to his other hand and looked down the length of the street. There were people everywhere. A posse of taxis went by in the street looking for fares, and then two rickshaws pulled by coolies, both engaged by old ladies carrying umbrellas. The two ladies looked like women from a Nationalist family, probably sisters. A clutch of amahs passing the time of day twenty yards from the Police Station on the other side of the road glanced at the two ladies and made a series of voluble comments about life, politics and money to another group of amahs coming to join them on their way home from the markets. The second group stopped and after a brief exchange waddled off together to find a tea-room. Fifty yards away on the Station side of the street, a group of European girls in the school uniform of St Paul's Convent stopped for a moment in front of a shop window to discuss the rising cost of make-up. One of them, a spotty blonde girl wearing glasses, touched at her cheek exploratorily and began an animated lecture on the correct way to apply mascara to fifteen-year-old eyelashes, to her two classmates. A man in a suit stood a little behind, partly obscured by the make-up artist, evidently waiting for them. Feiffer thought he was probably one of their Chinese teachers escorting them home. A group of Chinese youths on Honda motorbikes putted by the girls and craned their necks to see if there was a decent-looking Chinese girl among them so they could cat-call to her. There wasn't and they didn't. The girls finished their conversation and walked towards him with their teacher following a little behind, looking in the shop windows.

Feiffer looked down the road in the opposite direction. No one likely seemed to be coming.

The girls drew closer. Feiffer heard one of them say something in English about Max Factor and mutter something scholarly in comparison about Revlon. One of the other girls giggled. Feiffer looked around for their teacher as they passed. Their teacher had stopped. He was standing in front of Feiffer with his back to him, evidently waiting to cross the road. Feiffer took a step forward. It was late afternoon: his shadow went before him. The teacher said in Cantonese, 'Stop.' Feiffer looked at the schoolgirls. They were twenty yards down the street, still chatting.

The teacher said, 'Nice as they were, I'm not with them.' He said, 'I know you know what school they go to, but I was careful to keep just a little behind them. They didn't even notice me.' He said, 'I flatter myself I looked like one of their teachers.' He said over his shoulder, 'Have you got the money?'

'Yes.'

'Good.' Number Two said, over his shoulder, 'It's marked, of course?'

'Yes.'

'Yes.' Number Two watched the traffic in the street with interest. He was careful not to turn his face.

'Do you want it or not?'

Number Two did not reply. He watched the traffic. It thinned.

'Well?'

Number Two said, 'No. Can't use marked money, I'm afraid.' He said evenly, 'You're a policeman. Go into the bank across the street and change it.' He said comfortingly, 'They can always ring up Kai Tak to check, can't they?' He said, 'Of course they can.' He said, 'That is, if you want the place swarming with cops and falling aircraft.' He said, 'Go into the bank and ask them in a nice way to change it into nice, clean American notes.' He said, 'Legal tender in the United States

nd all its dependencies.' He said, 'Get on with it.' He said,
I'll even come with you.'

He moved his hand like a drum major turning a band and
directed Feiffer, at a discreet distance and at an opaque angle
to his face, to follow him across the road and into the bank.

9

It was a masterpiece of manoeuvring. Number Two went int
the bank ahead of Feiffer and ducked sideways to one side c
the main doors, standing casually at a counter. He scanned th
tellers' cages quickly, then turned away from them, still wit
his back to Feiffer. There was a giant Sikh guard wearing
khaki uniform with the bank's emblem on it and a blue turbar
The Sikh carried a single barrelled Greener shotgun. The Sik
glanced casually at Feiffer. Feiffer looked away.

Number Two said over his shoulder, 'Pick a nice friendl
teller and change the money.' He took up a deposit form an
a steel-nibbed pen and began going through the motions c
filling out the spaces, 'Don't bother remembering which pe
I'm using. I'll wipe my fingerprints off it before I go.' He sai
in a quiet voice, 'Apart from that, my fingerprints aren't o
file.' He said, 'I'm much too clever to have been caught.' H
said, 'I'll screw the deposit form up and put it in my pock
before I go.'

Feiffer looked around the bank. It was one of the fe
branches of the Singapore-China-Tokyo Bank in Hong Kor
and it had been built to impress. It was the size of a small rai
way station, with a high vaulted roof and deep mahogany woo
counters and furniture. There were wood tiles on the floo
highly polished, with the faint smell of furniture wax still risin
The place was spotlessly clean. The bars and mesh on th
tellers' cages seemed to have been rubbed by an army c
cleaners until they shone. There were half a dozen giant whi

roof fans on the ceiling, turning slowly at an unaltered pace throughout the year. The sombre atmosphere was broken only by the steady clicking of a comptometrist working at her machine and, from time to time from the tellers' cages, the discreet clinking of coins or the rustling of paper money. Feiffer said to Number Two's back, 'They're not going to do it.'

'Show them your identification.'

'I'd need the identification of Howard Hughes to get them to change this much cash without asking questions.'

'Then let them ask questions. You're a police officer, aren't you?'

'I'm a Chief Inspector. Which is not quite the same thing as being the Commissioner or the head of Interpol.' Feiffer said, 'Tell me which aircraft the device is on as a sign of good faith.'

'Since you're still holding the money you don't need a sign of good faith.' Number Two said, 'So far, the transaction is proceeding in the most civilised fashion possible.' He warned, 'Don't try my patience with obvious ploys.' He said suddenly harshly, 'That teller to the right will do. The one with glasses.' He turned a little towards the wall to cover the angle as Feiffer moved past him, then turned completely in the other direction. He caught sight of the Sikh patrolling the centre of the floor. He pivoted back a little towards the wall again to avoid the Sikh's eyes. He glanced at his watch. Everything was on schedule.

The teller said in English, 'Yes, sir?' and moved some papers to one side of his counter. He looked at Feiffer expectantly. He was a young man with bifocular glasses, keen to do well. He smiled one of his efficient smiles and gave the customer his full, complete, and utter attention.

Feiffer looked at him carefully. The teller appeared to be vaguely northern Chinese in origin, about twenty or twenty-one years old. Feiffer said, 'American currency. I want to change it into different denominations. Tens and twenties into one hundreds.'

'Into Hong Kong currency?'

'American currency. I just want to change the denominations.'

'Yes, sir.' There was no commission to the bank on that, but it was always good policy to help your customers with non-profit services. The profits came back to you in goodwill. The teller smiled a goodwill smile, 'How much, sir?' He looked down into his cash till to see how many U.S. notes he had on hand.

'One hundred and fifty thousand dollars.'

'—pardon?'

'A hundred and fifty—'

'For a moment I thought you said—' The teller smiled a non-goodwill, genuine smile of relief.

'Thousand.' Feiffer said quickly, 'Look, I'm a police officer. I think I'd better see the Manager.' He asked quickly, 'Is it still Mr Quang?'

'Mr—yes.' The teller glanced at the Sikh, 'Mr Quang, yes.' The teller moved his hand a little under the counter towards his Webley revolver. His eyes met the Sikh's.

Feiffer said quickly, 'Look, I know what you're doing with your hand, and I know the muzzle's pointed exactly at my midriff, but I really am a police officer. My warrant card's inside my coat. I'm going to reach in and get it.' He said soothingly, 'So don't do anything sudden that the bank might regret.' He slid his hand into his inside pocket and found the card, took it out, and laid it on the teller's counter. He felt something hard brush up against his side and saw the Sikh's shadow fall across the barred cage.

A voice speaking English with an Indian inflection said apologetically, 'My dear sir, did I accidentally brush you with the barrel of my shotgun? I apologise most profusely.' He looked at the teller and asked, 'Do I not apologise most profusely?'

The teller said, 'He says he's a police officer.' The teller said, 'He's carrying a gun. I saw it when he—'

There was that hard brush with the barrel again. The Sikh

said, 'Again, sir, I apologise for my apparent clumsiness. Reluctantly, with the current increase in crime, one becomes heavy handed in readiness.' He said, 'I might add to demonstrate this unfortunate state of affairs, that at this very moment the young teller's hand is nervously clutching a—'

Feiffer said, 'I'd like to see Mr Quang.'

The Sikh glanced at the teller. The teller scrutinised the warrant card. 'He says he has a hundred and fifty thousand American dollars to change.'

'Hmm.' The Sikh said helpfully, 'In that case, Mr Quang will be delighted to assist him.' The Sikh said, 'So delighted will Mr Quang be that I shall accompany you to Mr Quang's presence myself.' He said casually, 'I regret that I am so ill-practised with this offensive weapon that it may bump into you from time to time as we proceed to the office, but I am sure you will forgive me.' The Sikh said, 'This way. Straight ahead.' He glanced around the bank for accomplices and saw only a well-dressed man with his back to him filling out a deposit form quite obviously the respectable type. He said to the teller, 'Telephone Mr Quang that we are coming.' He said to Feiffer, 'Your suitcase looks heavy.' He touched Feiffer with the barrel of the gun.

Feiffer handed him the suitcase.

*

Dobbs said down the line, 'Who's this?'

'Detective Senior Inspector O'Yee.'

'O'—what?'

'O'Yee.'

'Oh, the Chinese-Yank-Eurasian—'

'Who the hell is this?'

'This is Dobbs.'

'Oh—yeah . . .'

'Oh yeah, *what*?'

'Oh—yeah . . . Dobbs.' O'Yee said, 'You again.'

'It's me again, all right! And it's *Superintendent* bloody Dobbs to you, you dirty little half-caste! I'm just making sure that your man Feiffer got the money!'

'Do you happen to mean Detective *Chief Inspector* Feiffer, Superintendent Dobbs—sir?'

'Has he got the money? Yes or no?'

'Who?'

'Feiffer, you stupid little—'

'Oh, you mean, Detective *Chief*—'

'Listen you—!'

'Yes, he's got the bloody money!'

'Then put him on!'

'He isn't here.'

'Where is he?'

'Who?'

'Feiffer!'

'He's out.'

'Out where?'

'I don't know.'

'—*sir*!'

'I don't know, *sir*.'

'He said the pick-up was going to take place late today. He should be getting ready for it. Making plans. Where is he?'

'Beats me.'

'Where's the bloody money?'

'What bloody money?'

'The pick-up bloody money—!!'

'Oh, that bloody money—' O'Yee glanced at his watch.

'Yes, you dirty little coon bastard, that bloody money! Where is it?'

'Oh, well . . .' O'Yee glanced at his watch again. 'Well, that's quite a long story, as a matter of fact . . .'

He wondered if Dobbs was taping the conversation.

*

Mr Quang said, 'Mr Feiffer—' He stood up behind his heavy desk and came forward to shake hands. He looked at the Sikh (for the sake of the continuing goodwill of the Bank) disapprovingly, 'Shouldn't you be outside on duty?'

Feiffer said, 'He was showing me the way.' He reached forward and took the suitcase and his warrant card. He said to the Sikh, 'Thanks very much for carrying the case.' He said to Mr Quang, 'Very helpful employees you have in this bank.' He glanced at the shotgun. It looked like a cannon.

Mr Quang smiled. He said to the Sikh, 'Thank you, Singh, I know this man.'

The Sikh nodded and went out.

Mr Quang paused. He asked, 'How can I help you?' He wondered why Feiffer opened the door a few inches and moved his chair back to sit half facing it. 'We're always glad to assist the authorities in their private transactions.'

Feiffer said, 'This is a professional transaction.' He put the suitcase on Mr Quang's desk with his warrant card next to it. 'There's a hundred and fifty thousand U.S. dollars in marked bills inside there. I want them changed dollar for dollar into unmarked bills.'

Mr Quang paused. He was a small Chinese in his middle fifties wearing a very expensive English suit. He looked at Feiffer's own less than very expensive stained white suit and looked dubious.

'It's part of an investigation. We'd like the bank to assist with it.'

'Naturally, you have the requisite authority from a senior officer?' Mr Quang leaned back in his chair. There was a rare nineteenth century panoramic sepia photograph of Hong Kong harbour on the wall behind him, a Dalton and Michaels original. Mr Quang said, 'From an Assistant Commissioner, or someone in the Government—or something?'

'No.' The photograph showed the island on a very misty day with clouds over the Peak. From the shipping in the harbour, it must have been taken in the late 1870s. Feiffer said, 'It has to be done quickly. It concerns the aircraft business at Kai Tak.'

'I've read about it in the newspapers.' Mr Quang said, 'A Superintendent will do.'

'The only Superintendent involved in the case is at Kai Tak. I need the money changed now.'

'I can telephone Kai Tak in an instant—'

'No.'

'Oh?' The mist around the Peak seemed to change before Feiffer's eyes into something beginning to resemble lethal radioactive fallout. Mr Quang asked deceptively pleasantly, 'Why should that not be satisfactory?'

'Because the Superintendent at Kai Tak would not want you to change the money.' Feiffer glanced out through the half-open door in the direction of Number Two's back. Number Two seemed to be looking hard at his filled-out deposit form and considering whether or not this bank amongst all others was the one to be entrusted with his hard-won money. Feiffer said to Mr Quang, 'I'm going to have to ask you to take me on trust and do as I say. It's a matter of doing it without question.' He looked at his watch. By now Dobbs could be on the phone to the Station finding out that the pay-off was in progress. 'Could you just do it now, please?'

'No.'

'Why not?'

Mr Quang shook his head.

'Surely to God you've got that sort of money here?'

'Certainly.' Mr Quang said, 'And we intend to keep it here. I'll telephone the Superintendent and if he says it's all right and is prepared to have you issue a receipt against his name that my directors will accept, then I might well consider it.' Mr Quang said, 'We just can't afford to go around handing over that sort of money on the word of—'

'Naturally I'll give you the money in this bag in exchange— it's perfectly good—'

'And marked.'

'Well, yes—'

'By whom?'

'Well, by the police—'

'So it's evidence?' Mr Quang said, 'The Singapore-China-Tokyo Bank earns no interest on money lying on judges' benches in Court.' Mr Quang said, 'I'll ring the Superintendent at Kai Tak.'

'I'd rather you didn't do that.'

'Perhaps not, but nevertheless—'

Feiffer said, 'Look, I'd really appreciate it if you didn't ring. I need the money now in order to—'

Mr Quang said, 'By a strange coincidence, we need the money too. That's why we're in business as a bank.' He said darkly, 'No one is suggesting that the money could be the proceeds of police corruption and that you could want unmarked currency in order to—'

'It's from the Kai Tak business!'

'As in Kai Tak from which there are numerous flights to Switzerland? As in Switzerland where there is no extradition?'

'It's the pay-off to the man who's been killing people!'

'Is it?'

'Yes!'

'Then I would suggest most courteously that the perfect money to give such a man would be money of the sort you already have in your bag, namely, money marked by the police.'

Outside the door, Number Two seemed to be getting fidgety. Feiffer said, 'For the last time, would you just take it on trust?'

Mr Quang looked at him.

'Please—'

Mr Quang shook his head. He reached for the telephone. He glanced up and found himself staring down the short black barrel of Feiffer's Detective Special. Mr Quang looked at it. His mouth fell open.

Feiffer said very softly, 'Don't touch the telephone.'

Mr Quang's hand moved away. Mr Quang looked down at the suitcase and the warrant card on his desk. Mr Quang looked back at the muzzle of the gun.

Mr Quang said, 'Just tell me what you want me to do and how you want me to do it.' His mind, according to the precepts laid down in Managers' Training School, began registering a full description for the police, then stopped. Mr Quang thought suddenly, "God in heaven, I *know* who it is!" He looked down at the warrant card with Feiffer's photograph, name and rank printed boldly across it and thought, "God in Heaven, he is the police!" Mr Quang said, 'I'll do anything you say in order to save lives.' He said, and swallowed, 'That has to be my first and only consideration.'

Feiffer nodded. He said evenly, 'Use the telephone to have your staff bring the money into your office.' He glanced at the photograph of the view of Hong Kong harbour in the nineteenth century and wondered how it might compare to that from Stanley Prison in the twentieth. He said quietly, 'Pick up the phone.'

＊

Constable Sun came into the Detectives' Room with the information that there was a robbery in progress just across the road. O'Yee said to Dobbs, 'I have to go!'

He slammed down the phone and ran down the corridor after Constable Sun, checking his revolver as he went.

＊

Auden slammed the phone down in the public telephone booth on Airport Road and came out of the stuffy space sweating. He said to Spencer, 'Nothing!'

'About the bodies?'

'About anything! There's no one there! How can there be no one there at a goddamned *Police Station*? It's our goddamned Police Station! Have you ever heard of there being no one at a *Police Station*? What if someone wanted to get in touch with them?' He said, working himself up into an orgy of irritation, '*I* wanted to get in touch with them!'

'Ring Kai Tak.'

'Oh, great! Why don't I just ring bloody Auschwitz and make a reservation for the gas chambers and be done with it?'

'Maybe we should at least try . . .'

'We *did* try! We got chucked out! Remember?'

'That was last time.' Spencer said encouragingly, 'This time at least we've got some real information for them—'

'And what if they ask what they're supposed to do with this real information we've got for them? What then? We don't even know what the hell's going on—how are we supposed to know how it fits in? Or if it even fits in at all?' Auden said, '*I'm* not bloody ringing them and that's flat!'

'I'll do it.'

'Wonderful! Terrific! Fantastic! Mr Popular is going to ring them! Get onto Munday and tell him in a sweet voice that you're the guy who threatened to remove his dentures a fang at a time! Tell him you're only trying to help—maybe he'll even offer to buy you a little drinkie-winkie in the V.I.P. lounge just to smooth things over! You never know, he might even have a little bit of cyanide left over to drop into your bloody teasie-weasie instead of milk and sugar! That good old bitter almonds flavour for the discerning sophisticated palate!'

Spencer said, 'That's arsenic.'

'Maybe he'll manage a bit of that too!' Auden said, disgusted, 'I'm disgusted. I'm going to go back to the car, turn on some pop music on the radio, and sulk.' He watched as Spencer went into the phone booth and rummaged about in his pocket for change. He turned back to Auden and smiled. Auden said, 'Oh, no!' He opened the door and handed him some coins then stood by the phone in dreadful anticipation watching Spencer's mouth move as he talked to Kai Tak.

Spencer came out of the phone booth. He said softly, 'Dobbs

is in closed conference with the airlines. Everyone else has gone to Yellowthread Street.' He grinned weakly.

'There's no one at Yellowthread Street!'

Spencer said, 'The Duty Constable at Kai Tak said it was about some money or other. He said he's been trying to raise the Station for some time. He said he couldn't raise anyone.'

'*He* can't raise anyone? *I* can't raise anyone! That's because there's no one there!'

'He said he could take a message for the Kai Tak people for when they came back if it was important—'

'What do you mean, "When they come back"? Where the hell are they *now*?'

'He didn't know. No one does. No one seems to know here—'

Auden said, 'What the hell's going on? Entire posses of cops don't just disappear off the face of the Earth!' He stared belligerently up at Heaven and shouted at the top of his voice in the crowded street, '*Where the hell is everybody?*'

*

The Sikh looked around at the armed policemen coming in through the front door and unlimbered his shotgun. Everything appeared O.K. to him. There had been that odd business of the detective handing out his suitcase through the manager's door to someone who didn't want his face seen, but in the banking business there were always eccentric millionaires who—The Sikh came forward quickly.

O'Yee said, 'Silent alarm, Manager's office!' He pushed the shotgun to one side, 'Which way is it?'

'This way!' The Sikh led the way to the office. The door was closed. He pushed it open and looked in quickly. There was only the detective and the bank manager inside. And the bank manager had said he knew the— The Sikh moved quickly to one side to let the police through.

O'Yee said, 'Harry—' He saw Feiffer's gun on his lap. The

ank manager looked relieved. He was smiling. O'Yee said,
There was a bank robbery—' He looked around. 'Are we too
ate? Is it over?' There were piles of American ten and twenty
dollar bills all over the manager's desk and on the floor. The
bank manager was smiling about something. O'Yee said,
'Where was it?' He looked around the room again urgently.

Feiffer shook his head. He said quietly, 'This was it.'

He looked with interest at the framed photograph on the
wall above Mr Quang's expensively barbered head.

*

On the phone, the Commander's voice said, 'Harry. I've got
a report in front of me from Mr Dobbs at Kai Tak. In it, Mr
Dobbs claims you accepted marked currency from his office
for payment to this Number Two character and—' He paused
as he read forward into the paragraph, '—and that you pur-
posely misled him as to the time of delivery.'

'Yes.'

'You agree that's correct?'

'I didn't happen to want Dobbs and his people blasting away
with shotguns again. I wanted Number Two to have time to
tell me where he planted the latest device and what time it was
due to go off.'

'I see.' The Commander read another section of the report,
'I thought I'd get onto you straight away, Harry, in order to
give you a chance to—' The Commander said, 'The report's
only just this moment come in. He further claims in it that the
information wasn't given. That is, the information from
Number Two in return for the money. Is that right?'

'He'll ring.'

'You mean he intends to ring up with the information?'

'Yes.'

'Is that what he said?'

'Yes.'

'I see. So, at the time, your theory was that it was best to

119

hand the money over without a fuss in order to save lives?' The Commander said, 'Is that a fair summary?'

'Yes.'

'You don't seem to be saying very much.'

'You've got the report.'

'Presumably your previous answer also covers Dobbs' next point about your being in a position to physically arrest him and not doing so?'

'Yes.'

'Hmm.' He read on. 'Did you get a good description?'

'He had his back to me all the time.'

'How did he manage that?'

'By the simple device of not turning around to face me!' Feiffer said suddenly, 'Look, Neil, I'm just the stupid mutt doing his damnedest to try to stop more people being murdered on bloody airplanes! That's all! I don't have any criminal involvement in any of this!'

'I know that, Harry.' The Commander said sympathetically, 'Look, I realise that all this is getting a bit personally upsetting for you, but I wouldn't take Dobbs' threats too seriously.' The Commander said, 'I had him on the phone a few hours ago and I've heard all this anti-Chink garbage and this business about your wife—'

There was no reply.

The Commander said, 'Look, Harry, I've known you for ages. I have to take these allegations seriously, but not as seriously as if I didn't know you.' The Commander said, 'As for this business about handing money over to criminals, well, if this particular criminal gives you the information as to the location and time of another device—if there is one—before it goes off, then it'll be worth it.' He said softly, 'God help everybody if he doesn't.' Feiffer heard him turn a page in the report. 'Dobbs also mentions that your man Spencer was rude to one of his people at Kai Tak. Get him to apologise, would you?'

'All right.'

'Fine.' There was the sound of another page being turned.

One of these days policemen might learn to put the main points at the head of a report, instead of listing them in chronological order. It might make life easier for ageing, half-blind bloody Commanders.' The Commander said, 'I don't think . . . there's anything . . . else.' He turned another page and said, 'Hmm . . . no . . .' He said, 'Suitcase full of . . . denominations of ten and twenty . . . marked by ultra violet . . . and handed to Detective Chief Inspector Feiffer by Inspector Ming of Kai. . . .' He murmured line by line, '. . . telephone conversation between Detective Senior Inspector O'Yee and. . . .'

He stopped.

He said, 'Omygod!'

The Commander's voice made a strangled sound. The Commander said, 'Uk—!'

In the Detectives' Room, Feiffer glanced at O'Yee. O'Yee stared at the ceiling.

The Commander's voice said down the line, 'Harry—?'

'Yes, sir?'

The Commander's voice sounded choked. It sounded throttled. It sounded as if he had gone red in the face. There was a gasping noise. It sounded as if—

The Commander shrieked down the line, 'YOU ROBBED A *BANK*—!!?'

Feiffer looked at O'Yee.

The Commander said, 'ARRGGHHH!'

It sounded as if he had just been shot through the heart.

10

In the Detectives' Room at Yellowthread Street, it was 6 p.m.
just getting dark. Outside, kerosene lamps were being set up on
open-air food stalls, and the smell of evening family meals being
cooked over charcoal fires came in lazily through the window
O'Yee said, 'What continues to astound me, Harry, is tha
you're not at this very moment in a basement room at Kai Tak
being soundly and expertly hit in the kidneys with rubber hoses.'

Feiffer glanced at the silent telephone on his desk. He said
'It could still happen.'

'The Singapore-China-Tokyo Bank got their money back.'

'The Singapore-China-Tokyo Bank got Kai Tak's money
back. As a matter of fact, since they only paid out a hundred
and forty-nine thousand on it, they made a profit.'

'I didn't think banks usually took a commission for making
change.'

'They don't. I more or less suggested to Quang in the course
of my all too convincing imitation of Jesse James that if he
took a small commission of a third of a per cent to keep his
directors happy, maybe nobody would mind too much . . .'

'A grand is considerably more than a third of a per cent of a
hundred and fifty.'

'I only suggested five hundred dollars. The other five was
his idea.'

'So, no charges preferred.'

Feiffer looked at his phone. 'It seemed like a good idea a
the time.'

'I hope Kai Tak are convinced.'

'Kai Tak aren't convinced.' There was a faint ding from the telephone and he snatched it up. It was Constable Sun at the front desk making a call. Feiffer put the phone down again.

'Is he going to ring?'

'He'd better.'

O'Yee said, 'I mean, you're absolutely certain there actually is another device on an aircraft somewhere?'

'No, I'm not absolutely certain there actually is another device on an aircraft somewhere! That's why I'm sitting around here waiting for a call! How the hell do I know?' He said, '—sorry.'

O'Yee nodded. 'What are the chances of the bank being allowed to keep it?'

'Keep what?'

'Their commission.'

'I don't know. Pretty good probably—I don't know.' Feiffer said suddenly, 'Christopher, this bastard is going to ring, isn't he?'

It was 6 p.m. The smell from the food stalls was very enticing . . . if you could manage an appetite.

*

The phone rang. Number Two said in Cantonese, 'Well, here I am: the richest shit in Hong Bay.'

O'Yee got through to the telephone engineer and gave him the number.

'It's me. The man of his word.' Number Two said, 'I thought since you'd been fair and honest with me it behoved me to be fair and honest with you.' He said, 'Which assumes of course that I am a man of honour who would not do anything unfair and dishonest to sully his reputation. Except of course by being responsible for knocking off several planeloads of people in the pursuit of unbridled avarice.' He said, befuddled, 'Which I am—is that right? In any event, I'm a little bit drunk which is just as it should be since I'm now thanks to you the riches' shit in town.' He said happily, 'Oh, the joys of financial stability!' He said, 'I'm rich!'

'Where's the device?'

O'Yee whispered to the telephone engineer, 'As soon as he changes phones I'll give you the number—'

Number Two said, 'Ha, ha, ha—ha!!' His voice sounded slurred and at the same time brittle. 'This is the last time I get drunk by myself. After this, I shall be forever in happier climes surrounded by success and sex.' Number Two said, 'A hundred and fifty grand wisely invested goes a long way.' He said, 'Pity about my Principal, but then he's a very understanding person. In fact, I telephoned him before I rang you and told him that since he was such a very understanding person I'd take all the money for myself and if he wanted any more, he could get it from you.' He said, 'He didn't understand.' He asked, 'Are you still there?'

'I'm still here.'

'The problem with my Principal, you see, you see, you see, is that unlike me, he's an ideas man. I'm the operations type. I do things. You see. I could tell you something I did that you wouldn't believe.' He said in a whisper, 'I'd tell you what it is, but why make it easy?' He hiccupped.

Feiffer said evenly, 'You machine-gunned six people to death in a disused water channel.'

'Well done! I did, I did. Which leads me to believe that my Principal is going to have to take my absconding with the money more or less, as one might say, lying down.' He said happily, 'You should have seen him. I don't know just what he thought bullets did to the hired help when they'd outlived their usefulness, but he couldn't hold it down. He turned green.' He said, 'When some poor old waterworker turned up by accident and I had to line him up and dispose of him as well, I thought he was going to puke.' Number Two said, 'The other waterworker—the one you might call the guilty waterworker—was kind enough to have suggested where four unidentifiably naked

124

bodies could be stowed. His stowage area was so appealing and well-chosen that I stowed him there as well.' He said, 'No wonder good help is so hard to find if they're all lying about in sewers.' He said chuckling, 'I may have caused a shortage at the cheaper end of the criminal help market that may last for years.' He said, enjoying himself, 'I want to thank you for all your assistance during this trying time.' He burst into laughter, 'I'll be away soon.' He said, 'Once you realise that there are people of considerably less worth than yourself in this world, it becomes diabolically easy to dispose of them in order to further your own prosperity.' He said, 'Don't worry, I promise to invest the money in an honest enterprise.'

'The device.'

'The device?'

'Where is it?'

There was a pause. Number Two hiccupped. 'I'm not so sure I should tell you.'

'You made a bargain.' Feiffer glanced at O'Yee. O'Yee was looking at his watch, timing the call. He seemed surprised that it had gone on so long. There was something from the engineer and he said urgently into the phone, 'Yes——?'

Number Two said, 'No, I don't think I will tell you.'

'Then there is a device?'

'Oh, yes. There were six bodies in the sewer, one grave-finder, one innocent, and four device planters.' Number Two paused for a moment. 'You see, the thing about people like my so-called Principal is that they're not prepared to get their hands dirty. So they leave it to people like me of a stronger disposition to take care of the details. So he doesn't know where the devices are any more than you do. It's all right for him to hide away while I do all the dirty work and fend off the cops while he just holds back and estimates things. Well, it's my estimate that things are getting a little too hot. So I'm taking his share as well. Common courtesy and a strong sense of revenge prompted me to ring him and tell him, so perhaps I'm not totally devoid of human feelings after all. No, on second thoughts, it was activated entirely by a sense of revenge.' He said, laughing, 'I must be totally devoid of human feelings after all, after all.' He said, 'Yes, I am.' He hiccupped. 'I don't think I'll tell you anything.' He paused for a moment. 'Except one thing only. Which is this: that solely in order to embarrass my now ex- and unnecessary Principal, —' He chuckled to himself, 'Again, motivated by all the basest motives, I reversed the order—make of that what you can.' He said, 'You're a good and honourable person, Feiffer, and you have a genuine concern for human life, so as far as I'm concerned, you can go stuff yourself!'

'I see—'

O'Yee began making urgent motions with his hand. He pointed to his watch.

Feiffer said to Number Two, 'You do realise, of course, that the current feeling at Kai Tak is that I'm in some way involved in your little plan—'

'Oh, yes. I hope in a modest way from my phone call to have amplified that feeling.' He dropped his voice, 'You have to realise, Harry, old fellow, that in this world if you don't have capital you might as well go out and put your head under a piledriver straight away. People like you never cease to amaze me. It must be some sort of character fault in people like you to think that you can trust people like me.' He said, 'You can't. If I had any feelings at all towards anyone they'd be towards the next man to come up with a good plan to extort money or kill people, or both. Since I don't have any feelings towards anyone, and I doubt whether there is anyone with sufficient nous to come up with another perfect plan in the first place, my feelings are totally non-existent.' He said, 'Pleasant as it is to have someone of your intelligence to talk to—someone else who doesn't mind taking care of the dirty details—I'm not quite out of the woods yet and I regret that I have to hang up.'

'First tell me where the device is!'

'Why? Because of all that suffering humanity?'

'Because you owe it to me!'

Number Two laughed. He asked pleasantly, 'Did you owe me a hundred and fifty grand? Did you? I damnwell took it!' He said, 'So if you want to find the device then I suggest you learn a few hard facts about life and go find it yourself!' He added in a heavily paternal tone, 'Nothing is for nothing in this world, Mr Feiffer, and anyone who thinks it is—'

'Then give me the name of your Principal—'

'Why?'

Feiffer glanced at O'Yee.

Number Two said, 'Why should I? Give me a good reason.'

'Just out of plain bastardry!'

There was a pause as Number Two considered it. Number Two said, 'Why not?' He said to himself, 'Yes, why not?' There was another pause.

O'Yee said softly, 'Fifteen seconds more on the same line and we've got him—'

Feiffer said into the phone, 'Well?'

Number Two hiccupped. Then there was a tapping sound, just once, as if something hard touched something else by the telephone.

O'Yee said, 'It's a public telephone booth somewhere in the area of—' He stopped and listened to the telephone engineer.

Feiffer said, 'Well?'

There was another tap and then a silence. Number Two said, a long way off, 'Look it was—' He was speaking in English. Number Two's voice said, 'You must be—' and then there was a soft sound like a pillow falling and then Number Two saying, 'Look, it was—'

In the earpiece of Feiffer's telephone there was a terrible smashing sound. It sounded like glass.

O'Yee said, 'We've got him! It's a telephone booth near the floating restaurant on Hong Bay Beach Road!' He said urgently to Feiffer, 'Keep him talking a moment longer and I'll get a patrol car out there!' He slammed down the telephone and began dialling the number for the radio room. He looked at Feiffer's face and stopped. 'He's still there, isn't he? He was there just a moment ago—' O'Yee said, 'Good God, we haven't lost him when we're so close, have we?' He said, 'I can get the area sealed off—'

There was a silence in Feiffer's ear, then a tap-tap-tap as the receiver at the other end of the line banged against the side of the telephone booth. There was another noise, a whistling, like air passing through a hosepipe full of holes. Feiffer waited.

O'Yee said desperately, 'What are you waiting for?'

Feiffer waited another moment.

Then the sound came.

Feiffer said, 'We're after a European with blood on him.'

'What are you talking about? Did he give you the location of the device?'

'No.' Feiffer said, 'You've got the address of the phone booth?'

'Yes—!'

Feiffer hung up the phone and went to get his coat. He seemed to be very tired and drawn, a man suddenly without hope.

The sound he had heard had been Number Two's death rattle.

*

At the front desk, Constable Sun said apologetically into the phone, 'In that case, Inspector Auden, I'm afraid they've gone again.'

'What, both of them?'

'They've both gone. Both Mr O'Yee and Chief Inspector Feiffer.'

'Then who the hell's minding the shop?'

'I suppose I am.'

'I mean, the bloody detectives' shop!'

'No one.' Constable Sun said in mitigation, 'They've gone out to a murder.'

'What murder?'

'On Hong Bay Beach Road. So Mr O'Yee said. All the other Constables are out there with them. The area's been sealed off.' Constable Sun said with an attempt at levity, 'If there's another bank job I'll just have to surround the perpetrators all on one side.'

'What do you mean, *another* bank job?' Auden said, 'Where on Beach Road? And who got murdered?'

'By the floating restaurant in a car park. I don't know who the victim is.' Constable Sun said, 'They're chasing a European.'

'What's that got to do with a bank job?' Auden said, 'What bank job? How the hell did the man get over to Beach Road? There *aren't* any banks on Beach Road.'

'The bank job was here in Yellowthread Street.'

'In—?'

'The murder was over on Beach Road.'

'So they're not related?'

'No.' Constable Sun said, 'Chief Inspector Feiffer did the bank job.'

'I thought he was fully occupied with the aircraft business?'

'No, I mean Chief Inspector Feiffer *did* the bank job.'

'You just said that!' Auden said—

'No, *did* the bank job—perpetrated!!'

There was another pause, then Auden said, 'Do you know, Sun, that around here no one ever tells me anything?' He said gratefully, 'You're the first person who's had the common decency to treat me like a human being who might happen to be interested in what's going on around him—'

Constable Sun said, 'Well, it's very nice of you to say so, Mr—'

Auden shouted down the line, '*And so far, I haven't understood one bloody word you've said!*'

Constable Sun said, 'Oh.'

There was another pause.

Sun thought it was the least he could do to start at the

beginning. He thought it probably did sound a little confusing if you hadn't actually been in on it as it was breaking. Getting it in bits and pieces *was* rather unfair if you had been out following up another job and when you rang up for guidance people started at the middle and just assumed——Constable Sun said patiently, 'Well, first, you see . . .'

There was a momentary pause——then, at the other end of the line, Auden slammed down the receiver in utter, speechless fury.

*

Under the arc lights set up around the bank of three telephones the smashed glass lay about like shards of ice. Light flashed back from the glass and from the windscreens of cars in the car park near the telephones. A flashing light from an ambulance fought a running battle of coloured luminosity with a rotating police beacon and there were more flashes of light from the buttons and cap badges of the uniformed Constables keeping the gathering crowd back in the car park.

Number Two's body lay half out and half inside one of the booths. There was smashed glass from the door all over his face and across his shoulder. He still held the suitcase, clutched across his chest in a dead man's grip. Parts of the suitcase were dark with blood.

Lying the way it did, the body looked boneless.

The Government Medical Officer, Doctor Macarthur, lit another French cigarette and balanced it carefully across the metal catch of his open Gladstone bag. He reached down and turned the head to one side. There was a tinkle as a sliver of jagged glass fell onto the roadway. A flashbulb went off as the Police photographer took a wide shot of the three telephones and then another tinkle as he ejected the spent bulb into his canvas bag. He moved around to one side of the telephones to try another angle for a general scene shot. Senior Inspector O'Yee was inside one of the booths looking at something and he waited until he came out and cleared the area. The photographer fired off his light.

Macarthur touched at Number Two's neck, turned it back the other way to get another view, and then let it fall back again. He touched at the neck with a stainless steel probe and then scratched at something inside it that made a grating noise. He leaned back, took an inhalation on his cigarette and examined the probe with interest. He sniffed.

O'Yee said to Feiffer quietly, 'The other two telephones have been vandalised. Evidently, he was too lazy or drunk to bother to look for another location.'

'Or too confident.' Feiffer watched Macarthur move the head from one side to the other. There was something shiny at the neck. Macarthur tapped it again with the probe and made a scraping noise against it. 'Any witnesses?'

'None. And your European seems to have got clean away as well. What makes you think a European did it anyway?'

'He spoke English to him.'

'Number Two spoke English to him?'

'Yes.'

'I didn't know he could.'

'Neither did I. From the few words I heard him say he seemed to have some sort of American or Canadian accent. Maybe that was why he was so adamant about not talking to you. Maybe he thought you would have recognised it.'

'Maybe. You didn't hear the European say anything?'

'No. Nothing.'

'Have you looked inside the suitcase?'

'Macarthur opened a section of it with a scalpel.'

'And?'

'It's the money. There are scratches and scuff marks on it where the murderer tried to wrench it free. Macarthur'll have to release it at the Mortuary.' Feiffer said, 'Evidently it means breaking a few fingers.'

O'Yee said, 'I checked the other two booths and the telephone books in them have the Yellowthread Street numbers underlined. Apparently this is where he always rang. He changed from one booth to another and from one number to another at our end.' He said bleakly, 'You can't accuse him of not being cautious. He must have rung the Principal from here before he rang us. How the Principal knew where he was—'

Feiffer said, 'The Principal was the ideas man. He probably picked the phones himself. Number Two was under the impression that violence wasn't in the Principal's line.'

O'Yee said, 'Well, at least, we've got back the hundred and fifty grand.'

'At least we've got back the hundred and fifty grand.' Feiffer said, 'That thing in his neck is some sort of knife. According to Macarthur, he was hit from a threequarters turning angle by a single blow that severed the carotid artery. The sort of thing that Commandos are supposed to be able to do.' Feiffer said, 'According to Macarthur, if you ever have an urge to murder somebody without making too much noise, that's the way to do it. All the noise of the glass smashing must have come as he thrashed about with it stuck in his neck. That accounts for the lack of blood. If the murderer had pulled it out the artery would have pumped out all over the place.' He said dismally, 'He was our only link with the device, whatever it is. The Principal was just the ideas man.' He said totally redundantly, 'Number Two certainly isn't going to tell us now.'

'Any identification?'

'No.'

'But it is the man you saw at the bank?'

'Yes.' Feiffer said, 'The device is going to go off or be activated or whatever it does, and for nothing—' He glanced back at the crowds forming. He said suddenly, 'And as for me now, well, I've had it.' He looked at his watch as an aircraft went over and shook his head. He looked up as Auden called across from the cordon, 'Harry—' and came across with Spencer.

Spencer said to O'Yee, 'Hello, Christopher.' He glanced over the dead mass at the telephone booth and nodded to Doctor Macarthur. He said to Auden, 'We should have thought he might be next.' He asked, 'Number Two?'

Feiffer nodded.

O'Yee said, 'I thought you two were wandering about asking people questions?' He asked, 'Did you get any answers?'

Feiffer said, 'How did you know it was Number Two?'

'Who else goes around bumping people off?' Auden said, 'He's making a clean sweep of the entire Agency.' He caught Macarthur's eye and nodded to him. He said to Feiffer, 'Not that anyone gives a damn, but we identified the fifth body.'

Feiffer said, 'What do you mean, he goes around bumping people off? Who goes around bumping people off?'

'Number Two.' Auden glanced at O'Yee. 'Number Two goes around bumping people off.' Auden said, 'You look a bit short on sleep, Harry.' He said to Spencer, 'Spencer and I are the forgotten men.' He said to Feiffer, 'I can't say I thought much of him, but it's a bit of a nasty way to go. Stabbed, was he?'

'What do you mean, you didn't think much of him?'

'Just what I said. P.K. Wu wasn't my favourite sort of—'

'Who's P.K. Wu?' Feiffer said, 'You mean the head man at the Cleaners' Agency?'

Auden said, 'Sure.' He indicated the dead man with his hand, 'Him. P.K. Wu.' He said slowly, 'You know, the corpse over there by the telephone that Number Two—'

Feiffer said, 'That *is* Number Two!' He asked quickly, 'What did you mean about making a clean sweep of the Agency?'

'I meant—' Auden looked quickly over the body. 'I meant—' Auden said, 'The fifth body was a cleaner employed by—by him. We found someone at the airport who knew him. He was—' Auden said, 'Are you seriously saying that that bland little bugger was Number Two?'

'*Where* at the airport?'

'In one of the service hangars—he hasn't been around for—'

Auden said, 'Do you mean, he was running a little do-it-your-self sabotage business from his office?' He said quickly, 'The dead man was employed as a cleaner in hangar number three, leased out to a charter company. He was working on one of the planes in for its regular service when he just didn't come to work the next day and—'

'Before or after the plane's service was over?'

'After.' Auden said, 'My God, do you think he—'

'Which plane?'

'Um—'

Spencer said, 'Flight 721 to Sydney, Australia. It's due to go sometime today.' Spencer said, 'I remember thinking—'

'Which company?'

'Pan Oceania Charters.' Auden said, 'My God, don't tell me that someone actually wants to hear what we've found out?'

'Have you told Kai Tak?'

'No, we haven't told Kai Tak. Kai Tak doesn't want to be told. We couldn't even get onto Yellowthread Street about—' Auden said, 'And what's all this business about a bank rob-bery—?'

He blinked as Feiffer and O'Yee ran for the car radio.

*

Seven minutes out of Hong Kong, over the South China Sea, the pilot of Pan Oceania Charter Flight 721 got the radio call. He banked his aircraft at ten thousand feet, dropped into a landing hold pattern, and began slowly circling over the city.

He looked at his chronometer.

It was an unwritten law of aviation that charter flights never left on time. It was an unwritten law, what with one delay and another, that they always got off the ground between ten and fifteen minutes late. It never failed. It was called the Departure, Death and Taxes Law. Like all long established laws, it kept you safe.

The pilot glanced at his flight log.

This once, uniquely, the departure had been dead on time.

*

On their way back to the car at the edge of the car park, Spencer said, 'There it is!'
The night was clear and coal-black.
It was a steadily blinking light in the sky, circling.

11

The interior of Flight 721 looked like a flying jumble sale, over attended. There were one hundred and nine passengers booked on the flight: they were crowded together in asphyxiating closeness in the forward section, pressed up against the closed cockpit door. They spilled into the galley and into the open door of the forward bathroom and up against the chill windows. There were rivulets of condensation on the windows—outside it was satin dark with night and several degrees below freezing. The passengers perspired under their freshly pressed light-weight clothes.

In the aisle in the centre passenger section, the Chief Steward paused and wiped his face with his hand. His neck was wet with perspiration and there was grime and dust down the back of his collar where he had undone his tie. He knelt down on the floor and continued wrenching at the tacks in the walkway carpet to free them. A row of tacks came loose and he moved across into the space between two rows of seats and pulled at the tacks there, rolled the carpet carefully, and checked under it and between the seats. Under the carpet there was aluminium flooring marked with innumerable scuffs and patches of dirt and grit. The Chief Steward moved adjacent to another row of seats and wrenched at another row of tacks under the chairs. They came loose with a series of sharp popping sounds. Behind him, one of the Stewardesses methodically slit open the upholstery on the seats in the uncarpeted section with a carving knife then ran her long fingers under the material for cavities. She found none in the current row of seats and went forward behind the Chief Steward to the next row.

Two rows back, the Second Steward and the Flight Engineer struggled with the retaining bolts on the tubular steel chairs themselves, using a pair of adjustable spanners. As the final bolt on each chair came loose they moved the entire assembly out into the aisle and studied it, pulled out the rubber backing, pushed it back out of the way, then went onto the next.

The Junior Stewardess had the passengers' hand luggage in a pile by the rear galley. Magazines and books, cartons of cigarettes and duty-free liquor lay in profusion in the aisle around her. She opened another paper carrybag and tipped out the contents. There were more cigarettes and bottles, a few paperbacks (she rifled through the pages and tossed the paperbacks onto the pile), a Polaroid camera (she opened the back, exposing the film, and checked the cavity), a few magazines, and a Thermos flask. She unscrewed the top of the flask and poured its contents down the galley sink, then upended the flask to make sure it was empty. She tossed it onto the pile. It made a tinkling noise as the glass broke. She reached the last piece of hand luggage, found it contained nothing except more cigarettes, and then moved forward to run her hands over the bottom of the luggage compartments above the seats to make sure nothing had been missed. She found a child's rubber toy—odd since no children were booked on the flight—examined it carefully, decided it was an artifact from an earlier journey, and threw it down onto the pile. It landed on a mountain of coats, each with all the pockets turned inside out.

The Junior Stewardess wiped her face, lost interest in the fact that balancing on upended chairs stretching up she was probably showing too much thigh, and slid her hand in to the next compartment. It was empty. She moved across the aisle and began on the other side.

The Flight Engineer nodded to the Second Steward that it

was time to halt on the chairs. They had gone half way down the length of the aircraft. The Flight Engineer produced a screwdriver from his hip pocket and moved back past the up-ended chairs to start unscrewing the panelling on the interior of the hull.

The plane was beginning to look like a schematic drawing of itself. The Flight Engineer unscrewed a plastic panel carrying decorative drawings of Bleriot's monoplane and looked in at the exposed hull. It was a mass of wires and junction boxes. He began examining each wire in turn.

The Junior Stewardess at the centre section closed a luggage compartment and went back to the rear of the aircraft to the intercom telephone. She was about to buzz the cockpit when the address system came on of its own accord. She halted by the phone and waited.

Captain Ford's voice said calmly, 'Kai Tak advises us that by now the seats and luggage racks up to the centre of the aircraft should have been examined. They now advise that emergency equipment is to be dismantled. Life belts are to be uncased and slit open for examination.' There was a pause and then he said cheerfully, 'There's no danger, ladies and gentlemen. We are not flying over water so we won't need them.' In his cockpit he wondered if there had been a ripple of laughter in relief. If there had been, he was too well insulated to have heard it. He said to his co-pilot, 'As soon as the rear section's clear we'll get the passengers down there so we can search the forward section. We'll leave the mess and get them to clean it up for us.' He said, 'It'll give them something to do.'

He made yet another slight bank to take the aircraft around on its fixed orbit and glanced at the fuel gauges.

The co-pilot, with nothing to do, looked down at his hands.

Captain Ford said, 'You hang on in here, Nick, just in case. O.K.?'

The co-pilot nodded and watched the mock-up of a little aircraft banking on the dial of the artificial horizon.

Captain Ford said, 'Just like Errol Flynn—'

The plane came out of its bank and he moved the stick to return it to level flight and adjusted the trim.

＊

The Chief Steward yanked at a section of panelling. It came away with a ripping noise and exposed yet another mass of wires and fuseboxes. He said in a whisper, 'If the Hong Kong cops knew there was something on board why the hell didn't they just catch the bugger who planted it and ask him where it was?'

The Flight Engineer, a tall American with a suntanned face and perspiration on his forehead, peered in at the wires.

There was a junction box just to the left of a relay that looked as if it hadn't been closed properly. The Chief Engineer unscrewed the cover and looked inside. It just hadn't been closed properly. He screwed it up tight and glanced at the passengers. They were silent.

The Flight Engineer moved on to a second box. It looked untouched. He unscrewed it and looked inside just to be certain.

The Chief Steward said, 'Well? Don't you think that's logical?'

The Flight Engineer sighed and went on to another box. He looked again at the passengers. The Flight Engineer said quietly, 'That was in another country. And besides, the bitch is dead.' He undid the four screws on the box and pulled it open.

The Chief Steward said, 'Henry, just what the hell is that supposed to mean?'

He looked around as the stewardesses began ripping open the emergency lifebelts and strewing kapok all over what had once been his clean, carpeted floor.

＊

'We've now cleared the rear section of the aircraft up to the centre row of seats. The hand luggage, wall panels, seats and lifebelts have all been checked.' Captain Ford glanced at his fuel gauges, 'We've got plenty of juice and the passengers seem to be in a sort of numbed state of acquiescence. We're in the process of moving them back to the rear to clean up the mess while the crew do the forward section. I assume the drill for the forward section is the same?' He glanced up at the radio dials on the roof of the cockpit and said, '*Over.*'

There was a brief pause while the static took over.

'Flight 721, this is Kai Tak Tower. Please hold. *Over.*'

'Flight 721.'

'Flight 721, the Boeing engineer here asks if you've checked the fuses and junction boxes behind the wall panelling? *Over.*'

'My Flight Engineer advises me by intercom telephone that he's checked the electrics on both hulls. Awaiting further instructions. *Over.*' He said quickly, 'Have you people got a plan of the aircraft? *Over.*'

'Affirmative, 721, we have a plan laid out on the plotting table.' There was a pause. 'The Boeing engineer has a complete set of drawings for the electrical system, seating arrangements, removable fittings, and the small motor mechanical and hydraulics systems.' There was yet another pause. 'The Boeing engineer advises me that the rear galley and bathroom should be dismantled and checked before moving on to the section of the aircraft beginning at the forward bulkhead. *Over.*'

'Are the police there? *Over.*'

'Affirmative, 721. *Over.*'

'Have they any idea at all what it is we're looking for? Do they know what sort of bomb it is? *Over.*'

'Negative, 721—' Another pause as someone must have said something to the operator, 'The police suggest that it may not be a bomb at all. Their information is only that it's some sort of device. *Over.*'

'Terrific! —*over.*'

The voice from the Tower said, 'John, this is George Yi

We met at an airport party a few nights ago. The tall bald Chinese you invited—at the height of your drunken stupor—to a sex and fun-filled weekend in Darwin. Do you remember? *Over*.'

'Darwin is very sex and fun-filled. *Over*.'

George Yi's voice on the radio said, 'I've reconsidered it and I'll take you up on your offer when this business is over. *Over*.'

'Do you have any good-looking sisters? *Over*.'

'Negative 721, the only relative I have in the world is—' The voice said, 'Hold, 721—the Boeing man advises that the roof panels could be dismantled by an untrained man and that there are cavities there suitable for the placement of an object. He advises your Chief Engineer that the panels are secured by Phillips head screws. *Over*.'

'Understood, Tower. I'll pass the message to him—' He turned to the co-pilot, 'Have we got any screwdrivers with Phillips heads on them?'

The co-pilot, himself an ex-Flight Engineer, nodded.

'We have the equipment available, Tower. *Over*.'

'The Boeing man advises that there is a second full set of tools available in the forward stowage locker. *Over*.'

'Roger, Tower.'

'—he advises that the locker—'

'Understood, Tower. We're a flying bomb. I'll have the Chief Engineer open the locker carefully. *Over*.'

'—roger, Flight 721.'

'Flight 721, holding in orbit over Kai Tak. Flight 721.' He turned to his co-pilot. The co-pilot's eyes were flickering back and forth.

The co-pilot looked at him.

Captain Ford said, 'Have *you* ever spent a fun-filled weekend in Darwin, Nick?'

The co-pilot shook his head.

'Ah. As soon as I tell the Flight Engineer how to reroof a Boeing, I'll be delighted to complete your education as to the strange erotic effect on females of hot climates.' He said, 'Just control your natural curiosity for a moment, and Uncle John will sit you down and tell you all—'

He pressed the Respond button for the forward passenger section intercom.

*

On the phone, Inspector Ming's voice sounded tight and strained.

Feiffer said, 'We can see it circling over the city.' He glanced at his watch. It was almost nine p.m. 'Has anything been found?'

'No, sir.' Inspector Ming's voice said, 'Everyone's up in the Tower with the senior personnel from the airport and representatives of the aircraft company. As far as I know, the Captain's taking it very calmly. They're dismantling the aircraft in flight, looking for it. So far, they've done the rear section and now they've moved onto the forward section. The aircraft's been up now for about three hours. The flight to Sydney is normally about twelve hours, so the current thinking is that if there's anything on board, it's designed to go off in about three or four hours when the plane would have been descending over Australia. If nothing's been found by then, it's been decided they'll have to turn out to sea in case of an explosion over the city.'

'I see.'

'The Water Police and rescue ships are standing by.' Inspector Ming said, 'The place here is beginning to fill up with relatives and friends of the passengers.'

'Do you want any assistance?'

'We've got two extra units from the Yaumati and some police women. They seem to be coping. Have you got anything more to go on?'

'Only what you know.'

'I don't know anything. Superintendent Dobbs and Mr Munday are in the Tower. How did you get the information? Was it from this man Number Two?'

142

'Indirectly.'

There was a silence. Feiffer watched the lights in the sky, blinking and moving into another wide circle in his window. Inspector Ming's voice said, 'In my opinion you acted very wisely giving him the money.' He said, 'He's probably gone to ground with it.'

'He's going to ground, but not with the money.' Feiffer said, 'Number Two was murdered by the man he called the Principal. We've got the money back.' There was a sudden silence, 'Are you still there? Has something happened?'

'False alarm. So the Principal's got the money?'

'No, we have. Number Two held onto it.'

Inspector Ming asked, 'How was he killed?'

'He was stabbed.'

'And you've got nothing more to go on? Have the lab reports given you anything?' Inspector Ming said, 'At this stage, anything might help.' He sounded worried. Feiffer heard the sound of an aircraft taking off or landing in the background.

'All we know is that the Principal is probably a European.' He paused for a moment and considered asking Ming for Dobbs' whereabouts at the time of the murder. 'The Lab reports say that death was virtually instantaneous and that the knife was covered in industrial cleaner as well as various other constituents that altogether make up something like glue with traces of tar on it.'

'A factory worker?' Inspector Ming said, 'Tar? Roadworks. Caulking boats? Any ideas?'

'Number Two was in charge of a cleaning agency. It's possible one of his people owned the knife. I've got one of my uniformed Constables around at Companies House trying to find out if he had any European backers, but so far no luck.' He said, 'If we get anything useful I'll pass it on to you straight away.'

'Thank you, sir.' Inspector Ming paused. He said suddenly, 'The people are building up around here. I'll have to go.'

'O.K.' Feiffer said, 'Good luck.'

'The same to you.' Inspector Ming said, 'Glue? And tar?' He suggested, 'Maybe a glue factory near roadworks? You've already checked—right?'

'Right. Glue comes from Taiwan. There aren't any firms making it here. And no current tar-laying operations.'

'Hmm.' Inspector Ming said, 'Goodbye, sir,' and was gone.

Feiffer glanced out the window.

The lights in the sky turned in slow, apparently unending circles.

*

The co-pilot said suddenly, 'I don't see why the hell we don't just put the aircraft down on the ground, get the passengers out the emergency exits, and then just let the bloody thing blow itself to smithereens!' He demanded, 'Whose idea was it to keep us up here anyway? Why the hell don't we just put the fucking thing down?'

'Like the last one? Without any wheels?' The pilot said quietly, 'On a full Pacific flight capacity of fuel?' He said, 'The other one was empty and it still went up like a Molotov cocktail.'

'Our wheels work! We've checked them! They've seen them down from the ground!'

'And the locking systems? Have they seen them lock in as well?' The pilot said, 'Listen, my old son, after six hours we move this hunk of junk out over the sea. If nothing happens, when we've got near enough to an absolutely empty set of fuel tanks, we'll go back in and land.' He said, 'The second I have to go out on the wing and piss into the tanks to keep the turbines going, that's the exact second to shuffle into Buffalo. At the moment, the crash foam they've laid on the runway down there is about four hundred feet deep. For all I know, it's so bloody deep the local Nepalese Yetis have come down for the skiing. On empty tanks it'll be like dropping into your old Granny's feather mattress.'

'So you say.'

'I do, me old mate. Your Uncle John is known far and wide for his dislike of hard landings and bony ladies. And I can tell you, quite truthfully, that so far in my long and varied career in aviation, I've never been killed once.' There was a buzz on the cockpit telephone and he picked it up and listened for a moment before replacing it. 'They've done with the rear and forward sections and they're starting on the forward auxiliary galley and the Stewardesses' seats.' He said, 'In a mere moment, this place will be crawling with more airplane dismantlers than you ever thought possible.' He said, 'Now, come on, me old mate, at this, the hour of our final and utter evaporation from things Earthly and employers lousy, tell me the truth: haven't you always wanted to see a jet airplane torn to pieces before your very eyes?' He said, 'Of course you have. Admit it. You can tell your Uncle John.' He put the aircraft into a gentle bank to complete a circle.

The co-pilot did not reply. He glanced out of the night black window.

'Ah.' The pilot said, 'In that case, the saga of a Darwin weekend, Part the One—'

He drew a deep breath to begin.

George Yi said, 'The pilot's an Australian named Ford. He's been flying jet aircraft since the mid-fifties and before that he was in the Air Force in Korea flying helicopters.' He turned a page in the dossier, 'He's even got a few medals.' He said to the Boeing man, 'He's a tall affable sort of individual with a practised line in being phlegmatic. Unmarried, no blots on his record, Senior Captain level, lives in Sydney.' He took up another folder. 'The co-pilot's younger and more excitable. Also an Australian, ex-light aircraft flying instructor, started life as a Flight Engineer, got his degree at night. He sounds all right too.' He asked the Boeing man, 'O.K.?'

The Boeing man, a short chunky American wearing a thin tie, nodded.

George Yi said, 'So if you're asking whether or not they're

going to lose their nerve, my estimate is that they're not.' H[e]
said darkly, 'I'm not so sure about the passengers, but th[e]
Captain's got them busy house-cleaning so maybe it'll be a[ll]
over before they have time to think about it.' He asked Super[-]
intendent Dobbs, 'You're sure this is genuine?' There was [a]
buzz as the R/T link to the aircraft was opened up again an[d]
he turned to switch it over.

He said chirpily into the microphone, 'Hello, John, every[-]
thing all right?—*over.*'

All the life belts had been destroyed in the search. George Y[.]
glanced at his watch.

It was time to order them out of the city.

*

At four ten and a half in the morning, the aircraft came bac[k]
into the city from the sea.

On the police and rescue boats, they saw it turn.

*

The Chief Engineer came into the cockpit and looked at th[e]
banks of instruments for a moment. He said without bein[g]
asked, 'The passengers are O.K. They're cleaning up the me[ss]
the crew left in the forward section and complaining like he[ll]
about paying a fortune to be menials. They seem to be workin[g]
up a healthy hatred for the Company.' He looked at the Capta[in]
and said in what passed in his Arizona mind for a broad Au[s]
tralian accent, 'How about two weeks in beautiful downtov[n]
Darwin now, John, me old mate?'

The Captain nodded. He said in what passed in his mi[nd]
for an Arizona accent, 'Takes a lot of beating, pardner,' a[nd]
asked, 'What about the galleys?'

'Checked. I'd say they were clean, but they're goddam filth[y.]'
The Chief Engineer said, 'How long have we been up?'

'Eleven hours.'

'Have you and Nick checked the hydraulics again?'

'And the control systems and the trim and the engines.'

'Then it's a hoax?'

The Captain nodded.

'How's the fuel situation?'

'Time to switch over to the secondary tanks. There's just nough to get us onto the ground and fill Nick's cigarette ighter.' The Captain asked, 'What sort of a job did the menials lo? Are the seats firm enough to get them strapped in?'

'Emergency procedure. We'll squat them down in the aisles.'

'Fine. Cabin staff coping?'

The Chief Engineer nodded. He looked past the Captain out he forward cockpit windows. Dawn was coming up in the east nd there were long shadows and pencils of light jousting with ach other on the flat land out near the New Territories and he Chinese border. He glanced at the altimeter: twelve thou-and feet, and then down and to the right towards Kai Tak air-ort. The Chief Engineer said, 'I had a date with an Australian irl in Sydney for this morning.'

The Captain made a mocking noise.

'—she's from Darwin.'

The Captain said, 'Time to get everyone in their cocoons. 'll get onto George at the Tower and tell him we're coming 1.' He glanced at the fuel gauges for the second time and said o the co-pilot, 'Do you want to crawl out onto the wing *pissoir* r do I?'

The co-pilot did not reply. He could see a long carpet of right white foam on one of the outer runways at Kai Tak. t seemed to stretch from the harbour's edge directly into dark-ess. He shook his head to clear the picture of it from his mind.

The Chief Engineer said, 'I'll go back and get things started.'

The Captain nodded. He flicked his console switch to hange to the secondary tanks. He looked at the co-pilot and eaned across him to flick the switch on the other console as ell. Dawn was coming up. He saw the mountains, and, nestling between them, Kowloon. The light was stretching across the farmlands near Lo Wu and Fan Ling and in towards the high rise buildings around Yaumati. He glanced across to the island of Hong Kong. Something about the lie of the land and the dawn reminded him of Korea. He thought it was probably nothing more than an association of memories.

He looked out again at the farmland in the New Territories.

The land was green and long-cultivated. Here and there on the hills you could see houses and roads and rivers. There were a few water buffalo working in the rice fields near Tai Po and here and there trucks going off to market loaded with boxes of produce.

Odd how land in Asia always looked the same. It had looked the same in Korea the first time he had been shot down by ground fire, and then the second time when a MIG17 had jumped them over a mountain range near—

Funny how it all came back in a series of sights and smells and feelings—like something suddenly reminding you that— Captain Ford looked down at his hand. He seemed worried about something.

There was a barely perceptible bump as the fuel from the main tanks ran out and was replaced a moment later by the kerosene from the secondary pods.

Captain Ford said, 'I seem to have hurt my finger . . .'

He looked oddly at the co-pilot and died instantly in his seat.

12

Feiffer held on the phone, waiting. He glanced at the wall clock. It read 9 in the morning. He looked across at O'Yee and Auden and Spencer. Auden glanced at his watch. Feiffer said into the phone, '. . . yes . . .' There was a pause . . .

O'Yee, near the open window, glanced out. He made a clicking sound with his tongue. He looked back at Feiffer standing at his desk and then at the wall clock. Outside, the traffic seemed to be still.

There was a long silence. Feiffer swallowed. He said into the phone, '. . . yes! . . .' There was a pause. Then Feiffer said, 'Is it? You're . . .' He said, 'Thanks very much . . . yes. Thank you.' He replaced the receiver gently on its cradle.

'Well . . .?'

Feiffer said, 'It's in.' He looked across at Auden. 'It's in.' Feiffer said, 'The co-pilot brought it in and there aren't any more casualties. Kai Tak Tower say that as landings go it wasn't too bad at all.' He rubbed his hand across his face and said, 'There's crash foam blown from the runway halfway to Singapore, but the Tower say that as landings go it wasn't too bad at all.' He said, 'The Tower say—' His hands were shaking. He said in a strange voice, 'Well, that's a bloody relief, isn't it?'

There was a silence. Auden released a breath. He looked at Spencer.

Spencer forced a smile. He shook his head and said, 'Huh.' Spencer said, 'Good old co-pilot.' He glanced to Auden for approval.

Auden said, 'Yeah.'

Spencer said, 'Good old co-pilot.' There seemed to be tears of relief in his eyes. Spencer said, 'Good old bloody good old bloody good old co-pilot!' He said, 'Yippee!'

Auden said, 'Tallyho, old bean, Hun in the sun, good old wizard prang and other upper class expressions! Good old co-pilot!'

Spencer said, 'Yeah!' He said, 'Whoopee!'

Auden said, 'Co-pilot for God!'

'Whizz bang! Rockfist Rogan! Wing and a prayer!'

O'Yee's face split into a grin. O'Yee said, 'Good old Charlton Heston in *Airport*! Good old American reference known to the entire civilised world as opposed to British reference known only to the British! Good old co-pilot!' He said, 'Good old Humphrey Bogart, genuine American actor impersonating good old fly-boys!' He said, 'Ha!'

Feiffer released a long breath. Feiffer said quietly, 'Good old Auden and Spencer for getting incompetent Chief Inspector out of bind by identifying fifth victim.' He said to Spencer, 'Thanks very much.'

'Think nothing of it.'

O'Yee said, 'That was the longest night I've ever been through.' He asked Feiffer, 'How many passengers were there on the plane?'

Feiffer said, 'One hundred and sixty-seven.'

'Jesus!'

Feiffer said quietly, 'Good old co-pilot.'

O'Yee nodded.

Auden glanced at Spencer. Auden said, 'Good old us.'

Spencer nodded.

Auden said grandly, 'As a genuine and authenticated member of the Hong Bay Supercop Squad, I propose to present myself to the FBI or Interpol complete with my chestful of medals and inform them that as the saviour of an aircraft full of crew and passengers, never dropping a one—'

O'Yee said to Feiffer, 'It's bad luck about the pilot.'

There was a silence.

Auden said, 'Yeah.' He said quietly, 'I was forgetting about him.' He said to the room in general, 'Sorry.' He asked O'Yee, 'Well, what now? No leads from Companies House about Number Two?'

'Nothing. Number Two's agency was strictly a one-man business.'

Feiffer said, 'That was George Yi on the phone from the Tower. We'll get the results of the post-mortem on the pilot as soon as they're in.' He said to Spencer, 'Does the combination of tar and glue mean anything to you in relation to the airport?'

'Tar and glue?' Spencer said, 'On the knife that killed Number Two?'

'Yes.'

'Do you think it's someone who worked at the airport?' He glanced at O'Yee. He said, 'You mean Dobbs?'

'Does it mean anything to you?'

'Not at the airport, no.' Spencer said, 'Are we starting again from the angle of the Principal? Did Fingerprints pick up anything?'

'No.' Feiffer said, 'We're starting again at the angle of the Principal. There's still one victim from the sewer you and Phil couldn't identify which means there may still be one more device. And so far, the Principal, whoever he is, hasn't got the money so we'll probably be hearing from him about it fairly soon.'

O'Yee said, 'He's a European, isn't he?'

'Number Two spoke to him in English.'

O'Yee said, 'And you think he's still got a final device up his sleeve?'

'I do, yes.'

O'Yee drew a breath. He blew another stream of cigarette smoke out the window.

Auden said, 'Where do we start?' He glanced at O'Yee's back.

O'Yee turned and stubbed his cigarette out in the ashtray on his desk.

*

In the sound-proof interview room at Kai Tak, Chief Inspector Munday turned another page in Feiffer's dossier. Something interested him and he read the entry for a second time, considered it for a moment, then turned over to the next page. By his hand, there was a folder containing the transcripts of all the telephone conversations except the last one. He made a mental note to ask Yellowthread Street for a copy. He closed Feiffer's file and read carefully through the passenger list on Flight 721 and then the records of the crew. Pinned to Captain Ford's dossier was a note to ring the Mortuary for the results of the post-mortem as soon as he could reasonably expect it to be finished.

He looked at his watch and wondered whether he should check that the Chinese Constables and policewomen were dealing with the passengers and their relatives. He thought they should all be done by now. He thought of ringing Dobbs to check. He thought Superintendent Dobbs was probably out with the crash crew and it would take a radio link-up with the aircraft to contact him. He dismissed the idea and took up the dossier marked *Investigations Conducted by Yellowthread Street.*

One of the silver buttons on his tunic was a little dusty. He took out his clean white handkerchief, carefully unfolded it and polished the button until it shone.

He refolded the handkerchief sharply and put it carefully back into his trousers pocket so it would not show a bulge.

He went on reading and thinking.

*

Feiffer said, 'We know this man Ip the Sniff was employed

by the people who catered for the airlines meals and we know he was placed there by Number Two's employment agency. We know that Ip was responsible for poisoning the food served on the flight and we know that the poison used came from the St Paul de Chartres' medical lab.'

Spencer said, 'And that Ip was one of the people killed by Number Two in the sewer. Number Two confessed to doing it.'

'Right.' Feiffer said, 'And that Ip stole the poison from the medical lab. Right? Or not?'

O'Yee said, 'It's a fair bet since the medical lab was broken into. All the other places: the caterers and the hydraulics people and the latest plane had men on the inside.'

'Supplied by Number Two.'

'Supplied by Number Two.' O'Yee said, 'Is it also a fair bet to say that the pilot on this latest plane—on Flight 721—got the last bit of that poison? It'd be a neat way of explaining how a man who has regular and thorough medical check-ups suddenly and inexplicably drops dead at the controls.' He said, 'But then if the plane was alerted no more than ten minutes after it took off from Kai Tak, how did he come to ingest it? Surely the first thing they would have done, going by past experience, would have been to make sure no one ate or drank anything.'

Feiffer said to Spencer, 'Bill?'

Spencer said, 'I don't claim to be an expert, but I always thought you thrashed about in convulsions with cyanide. From what you say, I get the impression the pilot just dropped dead on the spot.'

He asked, 'How long does cyanide take to work anyway?'

'A few minutes to an hour, depending on the dose.'

Spencer said, 'And do we know if he ate or drank anything?'

'According to the Tower, he didn't.'

Auden said, 'So it wasn't cyanide?'

'I wouldn't have thought so. What else kills you that quickly?

Other than being run down or shot or knifed or something?' He looked at O'Yee, 'Christopher?'

O'Yee said, 'I've heard that a bubble of air injected into a vein does it.' He said dismissively, 'There was no one else in the cockpit except the co-pilot. Why should he have done it? It's obvious that if anything happened to the pilot the co-pilot would have landed the plane. So why bump off the pilot and not the co-pilot with him? It doesn't make sense.' He said, 'If the plane was up in the air in a state of emergency for over twelve hours then it must have been something the pilot ate or drank before he boarded. I've never heard of anything that takes that long without any apparent symptoms and then ends that suddenly. Most poisons are carried in the bloodstream, aren't they? I just can't see how it could have taken that long to reach his heart.' He asked suddenly, 'Or are we completely on the wrong track talking about poisons? I got the impression that all the stuff that went missing from the medical lab was used up on the first plane.' He asked Feiffer, 'Wasn't it?'

'Yes.' Feiffer looked at his watch. 'We can expect the post-mortem result fairly soon.' He said, 'So let's leave that angle until then.' He said, 'The second job was straightforward: Lee, the ex-soldier, got a job at the aircraft servicing place and sabotaged the hydraulic system.'

Spencer said, 'And he was the one who supplied the machine gun from the Army.'

Feiffer asked, 'Which is now where?'

'I don't know.' Spencer said, 'The Principal was there when the killings in the sewer took place so maybe he's got it. It wasn't in Wu's apartment when Phil and I searched it last night, nor in his office.' He said, 'It's probably at the bottom of the South China Sea.'

Feiffer said, 'And we know that the last victim you identified worked in the aircraft hangar where Flight 721 was serviced. So we know that whatever happened to the pilot was caused by him.'

Spencer said, 'How? How could he have put something on

the plane that would have acted like that?' He glanced at Feiffer's face and said, 'Wait for the post-mortem results—right?'

'Right.' Feiffer said, 'But however all the jobs were done they presuppose that whoever was behind them—'

O'Yee said, 'The Principal.'

'The Principal—had a fairly detailed knowledge of the workings of both aircraft in general and Kai Tak in particular.'

O'Yee said significantly, 'Any suggestions as to who?'

'Just one.' Feiffer said, 'We know that the Principal knew that Number Two was double-crossing him with the money because he told me he'd already spoken to him and told him to get stuffed. The Principal, evidently a little faster on his feet than Number Two expected, came out and killed him. The Principal knew where Number Two was ringing from. The Principal was the ideas man. Therefore, it's pretty logical to assume that the Principal picked the spot for all that telephone-changing business, and that, possibly Number Two, since he was drunk and, to his mind, suddenly as rich as hell, simply forgot the Principal had his location.' Feiffer said, 'And since Number Two spoke to him in English, the Principal is an English speaker who knows about planes and about Kai Tak.'

O'Yee said, 'You're making a fairly convincing case for taking Dobbs out to the nearest tree and stringing him up on the spot—'

'Am I?' Feiffer said, 'The main reason Number Two spoke to me in Cantonese is that he had a strong American accent in English—' He looked at Auden and Spencer for confirmation.

Spencer said, 'He did, yes.'

'—and therefore, that would have narrowed the search down considerably. All this talk about adding despatch to the transaction was because Bill and Phil had been out to see him about his employment agency and the bodies in the sewer. He must have thought we weren't far away from linking him with the plane jobs. Evidently, he didn't want to deal with you that time, Christopher, in case, as an American yourself, you recognised the accent in his Cantonese.'

'It's a bit unlikely. I didn't pick it up on the tapes.'

'He was a very careful man. Or, at least, his ideas man was.' Feiffer said, 'Someone would have known that accents can be traced and that there are records at the American Embassy of everyone who's ever applied for a visa or ever lived in the States for any length of time.'

O'Yee said, 'Either that or he simply recognised my own accent when I answered the phone.' He said warningly, 'You seem to be painting a picture of Dobbs in very large brush-strokes—'

'I'm painting a picture of the person who bumped off Number Two and who was behind all the other—'

O'Yee said, 'Listen, Harry, there's no way Dobbs can make the mud stick to you, so there isn't the need for you to defend yourself against him.' He said, 'Dobbs is more than a—'

Feiffer said over the top of him, 'He's going to ring. I intend to be ready for him when he does.'

'Who? Dobbs?'

'The bastard behind all this. He's still got one device left and we've still got the money.' Feiffer said, 'So he's going to ring.'

O'Yee said, 'The Principal.'

Feiffer said nothing.

'I thought you meant Dobbs—'

Feiffer said, 'He's going to ring.'

O'Yee said emphatically, 'The Principal—?'

Feiffer said nothing.

*

The voice at the other end of the line said very formally, 'Chief Inspector Feiffer, this is Chief Inspector Munday at Kai Tak. The post-mortem report reveals that traces of a poison

156

were found in the pilot's body. There were residual concentrations of this poison on the index fingers of both hands. The poison was potassium nicotine. The report has just been delivered to us. You asked to be informed of the results.' He said without pausing for questions, 'The poison, which is lethal by percutaneous absorption, was spread on the switches in the cockpit that control the flow of fuel from the secondary fuel tanks. Normally, the switches would have been thrown just outside of the plane's destination of Sydney.' He said dryly, 'It would have been completely fatal for both pilots almost instantaneously.'

'Why wasn't it?'

Chief Inspector Munday said, 'Evidently, Captain Ford threw both switches himself. According to a statement from the co-pilot, the co-pilot was in some distress during the emergency, so it's likely the Captain did it in order to retain total control of the aircraft himself.' He said dismissively, 'We're not pursuing a line of investigation that might aim at implicating the co-pilot.' There was the roar of an aircraft engine in the background, 'At the moment, Superintendent Dobbs has detailed all available personnel to search other aircraft.' He said, 'I've given you the information you asked for. Is there anything else?'

'Potassium nicotine?'

'Yes. Taken in through the skin.'

Feiffer paused.

Chief Inspector Munday said, 'Well?'

'Thank you for ringing.'

The aircraft noise stopped, then Chief Inspector Munday said, 'By God, if you really are behind this you've just about had it! Superintendent Dobbs is going over all the reports and investigations with a microscope, and God help you if you're the one behind all these—'

Feiffer said, 'Thank you for ringing.' He glanced at the wall of the Detectives' Room. Something made a connection in his mind. He thought, 'Something Number Two said—'

Chief Inspector Munday said, 'Just so long as you know that we're—'

Feiffer said, 'He reversed the order!'

'What?'

'The order!' Feiffer said, 'He reversed it! The second last was the last!' He said, 'I know I'm right!'

But Dobbs; how the hell did Dobbs fit in?

He hung up on Munday suddenly.

*

Superintendent Dobbs opened the door to his office. He glanced at Inspector Ming by the desk. He said, 'All right?' Inspector Ming nodded.

'Well, don't hang about in here having a quiet cigarette, get back on duty!'

'Sir!' Inspector Ming stubbed out his hastily lit cigarette.

Superintendent Dobbs said, 'Disgusting habit.' He went to the ashtray even before Ming had closed the door and emptied it with a look of disgust into the nearest wastebin.

He looked at the pile of papers on his desk and took up the post-mortem report on the pilot, then opened the file marked *Investigation Conducted by Yellowthread Street*.

He sat down to read the two files with a curious expression on his face.

*

Feiffer said to Spencer urgently, 'Bill, what does the report on the knife actually say was found on it?' He began dialling a telephone number.

'It just says they found tar and glue on it—as well as blood and tissue and the usual sort of—why?'

There was a click at the other end of the phone and then the speaker identified himself. Feiffer said, 'Doctor Fahy, this is Chief Inspector Feiffer, we— Potassium nicotine. . . .' He said,

'Yes. I thought it might have been—' He listened for a moment. 'Tell me, exactly what aspect—' He said, 'I see.' He said suddenly, 'No! Don't say anything—it still isn't certain—fine. Yes, you do that. Just keep well away. We're just sorting out a few more things here and then we'll be— Good.' He hung up and said to Spencer, 'I know what you *think* it says. What I asked you was what does it *actually* say? Does it say tar and glue or does it say—'

Spencer found the page. He said, 'It says ". . . also found adhering to the blade were heavy traces of the constituents of glue—" '

Feiffer said, 'Not glue—the *constituents* of glue! Chemicals!'

'I don't understand.' Spencer said, 'And tar.'

'Tar?'

'Yes—!'

'Or—'

Spencer said, 'Tars. Sorry, it actually says t-a-r-s. It's the same thing, isn't it?'

Feiffer said, 'Is it?'

'Isn't it? You know, the stuff they put on roads.'

'How about the stuff research chemists investigate?' He said to O'Yee, 'That call a little while ago was from a friendly little birdie at Kai Tak named Munday. The pilot died from potassium nicotine poisoning.' He said, 'As in the stuff kept by researchers in homeopathology—'

'Like—Curry?'

'Like Curry.' Feiffer said, 'Like Curry the European. Like Curry the man who wants money for research. Like Curry the man who lost cyanide and only thought to report it when Doctor Fahy ordered a check of stocks. Like Curry the man who didn't even notice that his room had been broken into.' He said, his voice rising slightly, 'Like Curry, the Principal against whom Number Two said he reversed the order.' He said, 'He reversed the order because the medical lab at St Paul de Chartres is the only place in Hong Kong where there's potassium nicotine.' He said, '—the theft of which wasn't discovered because Curry replaced the stuff with something else to make the bottle look unused. He couldn't do that with the cyanide because his boss, Doctor Fahy, wanted a check done and knew already that cyanide was missing from somewhere. Fahy is a chemist himself. He would have discovered it.'

Auden said, 'But what about the nicotine? He would have found that as well.'

'When?'

'What do you mean?'

'I mean, when? When would he have found it missing?'

'Well, after this—after last night's business—' He said, 'How could he? It would have crashed into the sea—'

'Would it? Don't aircraft going down to Sydney fly over the land in preference to the sea? Don't aircraft always fly over land in preference to water? Wouldn't the Australian authorities have found it? They would. It might have taken time for them to find the poison, but they would have in the end.' He said, 'But why wouldn't it have mattered? *It wouldn't have mattered because the nicotine job was supposed to be the last!*'

'After they got the money!' O'Yee said, 'That was the last device to extort the final big sum out of us!' He said, 'Didn't Number Two tell you he was going to take a smaller cut?'

'And Number Two double crossed his Principal because, as far as he was concerned, all of a hundred and fifty grand was a damn sight better than a percentage of whatever the Principal was going to ask at the end.' He said, 'He reversed the order of sabotages so the Principal couldn't come after him. The last job, because of the poison, would have pointed exactly to Curry, but by that time, everyone involved would have been well away overseas and we wouldn't have been able to find them—'

Spencer said, 'Or lying dead in a sewer. Maybe Number Two could see something like that—'

Auden said, 'So it's Curry?'

Feiffer said, 'Right!' His phone rang and he picked it up carefully.

*

At the medical lab, Doctor Curry passed by the open door of Doctor Fahy's office. He glanced in at Doctor Fahy and stopped.

He saw Doctor Fahy's face.

*

The voice said in English, 'In exactly three and a quarter minutes I intend to change to another telephone. Keep all the lines open.' The voice sounded a long way off, muffled, indistinct. It could have been anyone. The voice said, 'Do you understand what I'm saying?'

Feiffer did not reply. He was aware that his hand was gripping the receiver in anticipation. He heard O'Yee pick up his own telephone and start to ring the Engineers for a trace. Feiffer shook his head.

The indistinct voice said, 'Are you there?'

Feiffer said carefully, 'Yes, I'm here. I'm very glad to be able to speak to the man in charge at long last.'

The voice said nothing. The voice said, 'Things are beginning to go a little wrong and I want the money now.' The voice said, 'There's another device and I want the money now.'

'I see.' Feiffer said, 'I think that can be arranged.' O'Yee's telephone rang and he picked it up quickly and spoke into it. Feiffer said to the voice, 'I was wondering how long it would take you to surface after you killed Number Two.'

The voice said, 'You've got the wrong person.'

'Have I?'

'Yes.'

Feiffer said sarcastically, 'The Principal? Haven't I got the—'

The voice said, 'No.'

'Oh?'

The voice said, 'No.' It said, 'The Principal, like Number Two, is expendable.' The voice said, 'This time you're talking to the man in charge.' The voice said evenly, so muffled as to be almost indistinct, 'This is Number One.'

'Listen, you—'

The voice said, 'The money!'

O'Yee hung up the other phone. He came over quickly and said, 'He's been alerted!' He said quickly, 'That was Fahy— Curry's taken off in the medical lab building! I told Fahy to evacuate the building in case he's still got the machine gun! Fahy's closed all the doors. Curry's somewhere on the third floor!' He said suddenly looking at the phone in Feiffer's hand, 'My God, Fahy said there weren't any telephones up there!'

Feiffer said, 'What?' He lowered the phone for a moment. 'Whoever you're talking to, it's not Curry!' He glanced at the exposed mouthpiece of the phone, pointing directly at him and said, 'My God, he didn't hear me, did he?' He said in horror, 'I thought you still had the—'

The line went dead.

O'Yee said, 'Did he hear me?' He said, 'He knows we're—' He said suddenly, 'If there aren't any telephones where Curry is how can he be the Principal? If the—'

Feiffer said, 'It was Number One. Get a car, quickly! It was the man in charge who knows all about airplanes and airports and who planned the whole thing. It was the man who would have known people like Number Two.' He said, 'And he knows we know that the Principal is Curry.' He said, 'And you can bet your life that the Principal knows exactly who *he* is! He said, 'Number One's been sitting back directing the whole course of this business from the start while his underling go on with the job of supplying the lethal tools and, in turn, his underling got on with the job of using them!' He said to Auden, 'You ring Kai Tak as fast as you can and tell me what you find out!' He said, 'Just find out one thing: whether there's anyone there or not. And by anyone, I mean—' He looked at O'Yee's face and said at the end of his patience, 'Fo

Christ's sake, Christopher, admit it! It's Dobbs!' He said as O'Yee contacted the garage for the car, 'It's got to be!' He looked at Auden on the phone.

Auden hung up. 'That was Munday. Dobbs isn't there. Munday says he doesn't know where he is—'

Feiffer said, '*I* know!'

'Where?'

Feiffer looked at him for a moment. It all fitted. All of it. He said suddenly, 'He's gone out to the medical lab to kill Curry!' He shouted at O'Yee on the other phone, '*Where the hell's that bloody car?*'

13

Doctor Fahy was standing alone on the white cement steps of the four-story medical lab building in the grounds of the hospital. A giant Jumbo jet on its way to the airport roared over the building at an altitude of a few hundred feet with its undercarriage coming down. Feiffer looked quickly up at it. The underbelly of the plane looked silver and thick with people. He reached Fahy at the top of the stairs and looked in through the glass door behind him. The foyer hall inside was empty. O'Yee, at the bottom of the steps, glanced down the sides of the building and motioned urgently for Auden and Spencer to cover the rear. He came up the steps two at a time. He said to Fahy, 'You said on the phone that you'd evacuated the building. Have you done it?'

Fahy nodded. He looked worried.

'And Curry is where?'

'On the third floor. One of my people saw him running down the corridor. I've had the elevators turned off and the stairs have automatically closing fire doors on them.' Fahy said, 'He's trapped up there.' He glanced with concern at O'Yee. He saw the flash of something steel and lethal in a leather shoulder holster under O'Yee's coat. He said, 'Look, I—' He glanced up and down the length of the building to make sure everyone had been evacuated from the area. He said to O'Yee, 'Did he really kill all those—'

Feiffer said, 'The other one. Where is he?'

'What other one?'

O'Yee said, 'Mr Feiffer and I want the keys to the elevator and to the fire doors and a master key to all the rooms.' He asked, 'What's on the third floor?'

'Nothing. The acid room. It's where we store bulk quantities of corrosives. It's just under the generator room. It was always too noisy to work there.' Doctor Fahy said, 'We've got an application in for funds to insulate the ceiling against the noise, but so far we—'

Feiffer said, 'There were two of them and I'm still waiting to hear where the other one is.'

'What do you mean?'

Feiffer said, 'I mean, the other one!' He asked Fahy roughly, 'Who else is in there?'

'Just your other man and Curry. There's no one else at all.'

O'Yee said, 'What other man?'

Feiffer said, 'Dobbs.' He touched the butt of his Detective Special and slipped off the retaining hammer loop from the holster.

Fahy said, 'I don't know his name. He turned up just a little before the evacuation—' Fahy said, 'We got everyone out. There was a traffic policeman in the street and he—' He said, 'I assumed the other one was with you.'

'Where is he now?'

'I don't know.'

'Did he know where Curry was? Did you tell him?'

'Yes—I think so. No. I don't know. He was seen on the stairs just after the traffic policeman came in to help. I just assumed—'

O'Yee said, 'How did you know the second man was a policeman?'

Feiffer looked at Fahy. 'Because he was wearing a bloody shiny uniform—right?'

'Yes.' Doctor Fahy said, 'I just thought—after all he was a European in full uniform. A Chief Inspector or something—'

Feiffer said, 'A Superintendent.'

'Was he?' Fahy said, 'Was he with you? I just assumed—'

Feiffer said to O'Yee, 'You stay here and cover the front doors.'

'I'm going up with you!'

'You seal off the main entrance and get Doctor Fahy away.' He said with a strange look in his eyes, 'I'll take care of our friend Curry.' He glanced at Fahy and took the keys from his hand.

'And what about Dobbs?'

Feiffer glanced at him. 'And I'll bloodywell take care of Dobbs as well.' He suddenly snapped, 'Just you make sure you stay here! All right? And that includes bloody Auden and Spencer too! And it also happens to be an order! Right?'

'Listen, Harry—'

Doctor Fahy glanced at them both.

Feiffer said, 'Which one's the key to the main doors?' He held out the keys.

'That one. The smaller one is for the elevators.'

'Fine.'

O'Yee said ominously, 'Now look, Harry, you're not Buck Rogers in the goddamned 23rd Century—'

'No, I'm the bloody mastermind! Remember?'

'You're not in the right frame of mind for—'

'Don't you tell me about bloody frame of mind! I'm the poor mutt that bastard up there was going to throw to the fucking wolves! Remember?'

'And what the hell do you think you're going to do?' O'Yee wished Fahy hadn't been there. He wanted to say something to Feiffer about witnesses. That would have made it even worse. He said, 'And just what the hell do you propose to do?'

Feiffer drew his short barrelled revolver. He went towards the door and unlocked it with the first key. O'Yee went after him.

O'Yee said, 'Well?'

Feiffer said, 'Get to your post!' He pushed open the door, went inside the foyer hall, and locked the door again from the inside.

He went very firmly and decisively towards the row of elevators and inserted a key into the central console.

*

Fahy said, 'Listen, I assume that this is all right?'

O'Yee did not reply.

'I mean, is that the way police officers are supposed to go on? I mean, I got the distinct impression that—'

O'Yee's eyes stayed on him. They seemed to be seeing something else. O'Yee said, 'You'd better clear the area.'

Fahy said anxiously, 'Look, shouldn't you go in and—I mean—'

O'Yee looked at him. He said suddenly, 'Please, just give me a moment to think.'

The moment kept eluding him.

*

The elevator door opened on the third floor. It stayed open. Feiffer had broken the lightbulb with his gun butt and he stayed inside the elevator in the darkness. The corridor was dim and empty. It smelled unused. He could hear the noise from the generators on the floor above, a steady humming vibration. The gun in his hand was light and steady. He waited. His breath came in a steady, shallow rhythm. He looked straight ahead down the corridor. There was a muscle at the corner of his mouth. It was tight and tensed hard.

He waited and watched with the steady humming in the background.

*

Auden said, 'You let him go in alone? Are you crazy?'

'He *wanted* to go in alone! What was I supposed to do— beat his head in and take command of the fucking *Bounty* on the spot? What the hell do you expect me to do? He's the bloody senior officer, not me!' O'Yee demanded, 'And what the hell are you doing around here at the front? You're supposed to be with Spencer covering the rear!'

'There isn't any bloody rear. It joins onto the hospital. There's one fire door at the back and that's been automatically shut with a bloody great bolt on the inside!' Auden said, 'How the hell did you let him go up there by himself? Get the bloody key and—'

'There isn't any key! He's got the only other key there is!'

'Well then smash the fucking door down!' Auden said, 'What if he kills Dobbs on the spot and then goes on to bump off Curry as well? Where the hell are the witnesses?'

'He isn't going to kill anyone!'

'Oh, great! How do you know that? By bloody Chinese telepathy? How the blue blazes do you know he isn't going to—'

'Because I bloody know *him*!'

'Then why the hell's he gone in by himself?'

'Maybe to keep us out of it!'

'Right!'

'I mean to keep us out of something between him and Dobbs!' O'Yee said, 'I mean, to keep us out of the shit Dobbs is trying to pile on—'

'You really believe that?'

'Yes!'

'Who is he supposed to be? Bloody creamy white Detergent-cop?' Auden said, 'You must be out of your tiny bloody—'

O'Yee said, 'I know him! I've known him for years! He wouldn't!'

'From what I hear Dobbs was only two steps away from busting down the door of his home and raping his wife and kids! What the fucking hell would you do!'

'*All right*!'

'All right *what*?'

O'Yee paused. He glanced up at the four-story building. He clenched his fist.

'Well?'

O'Yee said, 'All right. Get the Kai Tak cops over here.'

'What about the door?'

'Kai Tak. All right?'

'And a couple of squads of the Emergency Unit. They can have that bloody bit of glass and aluminium off its hinges in about two seconds flat—'

O'Yee's face constricted. He looked hard at Auden.

Auden said, 'Well?'

'Do what you're damnwell told!' O'Yee shouted at him, 'You goddamned insubordinate motherfucker, just ring the Kai Tak cops and no one else!' He shouted almost at the top of his voice, '*All right?*'

For an instant, Auden drew back his fist. He changed his mind. He glanced up at the building.

O'Yee said, 'Well? *Do it!*'

Auden said, 'Yes, *sir*!!'

He ran towards the car, cursing and muttering to himself.

*

Feiffer unscrewed the last lightbulb from the corridor roof. There was only one more door in the small corridor. The door was unlocked. Without the lights he could not be seen in silhouette in the corridor. There was a light on in the room: he could see it under the door. The steady humming of the generators on the floor seemed to be getting louder.

He pushed the door open very slowly with the barrel of his gun and saw Dobbs.

*

Auden looked across from the car seat at O'Yee. O'Yee was at the glass doors at the top of the cement stairs. He had his hand on the door, pushing it. He didn't seem able to decide about something. He glanced back. Auden said into the car radio, 'All I know is that you've been asked to assist—' He said, 'Your man Dobbs is on the scene. All right?' He said as an afterthought, 'Over.'

Munday said back, 'I haven't got my full strength available—they're all over the airport—it'd take hours to round them all up and—'

'Then just come yourself! All right?'

'It's not all right! There are regulations about—'

'Stuff the regulations!'

Auden glanced at O'Yee. He looked like a little boy trying to get into a birthday party without an invitation. He flicked the R/T button to RECEIVE and got a burst of thick static.

Auden glanced at O'Yee. He snapped the button on the radio to OFF and went across.

*

Feiffer's voice said out of the darkness, 'Mr Dobbs, my name is Feiffer.' His voice said evenly and calmly from the abyss of the black corridor, 'I promise you that if your hand moves even one millimetre towards your gunbelt I'll blow your head straight off your shoulders without a second's hesitation.' There was a zinc bath against one wall, next to a row of enormous glass bottles full of acid. Some of the acid was bubbling from a glass tube into the zinc bath and giving off pungent fumes.

Feiffer's voice said very evenly as he stepped into the lit room, 'Just keep very, very still and don't say anything.'

*

O'Yee was wrenching at the door. There seemed to be tears in his eyes. He said to the door, 'Goddammit! Goddammit!' He wrenched at the door like a maniac and shouted at the door, 'Bloody Christ!' He turned around to Auden.

O'Yee shouted at him, 'Get the fucking Emergency Unit to get the door down!'

He wrenched at the door and shouted, '*Goddammit*!!'

*

Dobbs said, 'It wasn't me!'

Feiffer looked at the body on the floor. It was Curry. There was a terrible slash wound across his throat. Blood had bubbled out on the bare floor and across his hands as if he had tried to claw it back into his body and there was a trail of blood in a little semi-circle where he had pivoted around trying to find all the blood and put it back in. His eyes were open and glazed in dead horror. Next to him, a cupboard door was open. Strewn around the open door were airtickets and currency: giant coloured Swiss francs. There was a half-open passport, drenched in blood. Dobbs said, 'I didn't kill him!' He said suddenly, 'Feiffer!' He stood up with his eyes suddenly coming back to life. 'You *bloodywell* did it and I can prove it!'

Feiffer said quietly, 'If you take a step towards me, it'll be your last.'

'Go ahead then! Fucking kill me! Kill me here and then try and talk your way out of it! Where are your people?'

Feiffer said nothing.

'You're here by yourself! On your own account!' Dobbs shrieked, 'Go on then! Fucking bump me off and try and explain that one!' He took a step forward. He was an enormous man with red hair, in his fifties.

'Don't . . .'

Dobbs shouted, 'He was the Principal! Him! Curry!'

Feiffer did not reply.

'And you're the man above him!'

The gun in Feiffer's hand held steady.

'The big European boss man! The man who gives all the orders to the stupid fucking Chinks and to this stupid bastard! The bloody ideas man! You murdering bastard, you! You killed almost ninety people!' His voice began to rise, 'You dirty, lousy murdering—'

Feiffer said, 'You killed them, not me. You're the one wit̶ all the knowledge of aircraft and airports. You're the ma̶ who knew people like Wu. You're the man who rang me an̶ realised it had all gone wrong.' He said decisively, 'And you'r̶ the man standing over the body of the Principal.' He sai̶ 'Dobbs, I'm going to put you away in Stanley Prison for th̶ next two hundred and fifty-nine years—'

'Don't you hand me that shit!! You're going to kill me an̶ we both know it! You're full-time in the killing busines̶ Feiffer! You knew once I got that post-mortem report, I'̶ realise who was supplying your bloody poison and by Go̶ you made sure you were here just ahead of me to kill yo̶ goddamned Principal first! What's the bloody little leth̶ programme this time? Bump me off with my own gun and stic̶ it in Curry's hand so it looks like we killed each other? Wel̶ you've made one big mistake about that! I'm not going to han̶ over my gun to you or anyone else, and the only way you'r̶ going to get it from me is to kill me with your own gun an̶ by God, when they find a .38 in me, you're going to be th̶ first person Munday has on his way to Ballistics!' He sai̶ 'They've still got hanging in this bloody Colony, thank Go̶ and they're going to string you up so high the drop'll tear yo̶ fucking head off!' He said, 'I wish to Christ I could come bac̶ and see it!'

Feiffer said quietly, 'I charge you with the murder of a num̶ ber of persons to be specified, that on certain dates, you di̶ with malice aforethought—'

'You must be out of your mind!'

'—and I caution you that anything you may say may late̶ be given in evidence against you—'

Dobbs said, 'How are you going to explain the fact that yo̶ were here at all? You didn't get a copy of the post-morte̶ report on the pilot so how did you know to come here?' Dobb̶ said, 'That man was a friend of mine, you lousy bastard—'

Feiffer paused. He said, 'Munday gave it to me.'

'Oh, sure!'

Feiffer said, 'And then I rang Doctor Fahy to check if—'
He asked, 'Did you speak to Fahy on your way here—?' He
said, 'You did. Fahy said you were in the building and—'
Feiffer said suddenly, 'If you didn't do it, then why the hell
did you kill Curry?'

'I didn't kill *anybody*!' Dobbs said, 'Look at me for Christ's
sake! That stupid sod's had his throat cut! Where the hell's
the blood all over me if I cut his bloody throat?' He said, 'For
Christ's sake, do you think I'd be stupid enough to turn up in
full uniform if I was going to kill someone?'

'You rang me! You said you were Number One!'

'How could I say I was a bloody dead Chink!'

'Not Number Two, Number bloody *One*!'

'I don't know what you're fucking talking about!' Dobbs
said, 'Listen, Feiffer, if you're going to kill me, you'd better
get on with it, because in about two seconds flat I'm coming for
you and if I can get just one of my hands around your bloody
throat before you squeeze off a shot, I promise you will never
get it loose!'

'What the hell's the acid bath on for?'

'It was on when I got here! And Curry was dead when I
got here! I was just about to search for the man who did it
when you walked in!' Dobbs said, 'I don't have to search any
more, do I?' Dobbs said, 'He was killed a couple of minutes
before I got here—so where did you hide?'

Feiffer said, 'I came in from the corridor.' He said curiously,
'There isn't anywhere to hide.' He looked around the room
for the coat Dobbs had worn to protect himself from the blood.
There was no coat. He looked at the acid bath.

Dobbs said in a strange voice, 'If it wasn't you, then who
the hell was it?' He looked down at Curry. 'And who the hell
killed him?' He looked at Feiffer. 'It was you.' He asked,
'Where's the machine gun?'

Feiffer looked at the acid bath.

Dobbs said, 'There's nowhere to hide out in the corridor and
all the elevators are locked.'

173

'Then how did you get here?'

'The stairs. The fire doors stop at the second floor.' Dobbs said, 'I came up the stairs. There was someone already here who'd been in the building before me.' He said, 'If the elevators were locked on all the floors, why the hell didn't I see you on the stairs if you were behind me?' He said, 'How did you get up here?'

'I got the key from Fahy.'

'After the doors were locked?'

'Yes.'

Dobbs paused. After a moment he said softly, 'It wasn't you, was it?'

'No.'

Dobbs said, 'It wasn't you.'

Feiffer lowered his gun. The noise of the generators was an incessant hum.

Dobbs said, again, 'If it wasn't you, then who the hell was it?' He said, 'If you didn't come here to kill Curry, then who the hell did?'

Feiffer said, 'Someone rang me for the money. I thought it was you.'

'When?'

'About an hour ago.'

'It takes three quarters of an hour to drive here from Kai Tak. Fahy can tell you that I've been in the building for over half an hour.' Dobbs said, 'It couldn't have been me.' He said, 'Whoever killed Curry was going to drop his body into the acid bath and dispose of it—'

There was a little storeroom door to one side of the acid vats, in the corner of the room. The door swung open on its hinges. A voice from the storeroom said very steadily, 'As much as I may have enjoyed listening to you both, I regret the time for talk is now over.' He cautioned Feiffer, 'Don't raise that revolver Mr Feiffer, or I shall have to use this sub-machine gun now—' He stepped out of the storeroom holding the Sterling in his hands. He said, '—rather than, sadly, just a little later.' He said cheerily, 'Mr Dobbs, in your closed little world, will wonders never cease?' He looked at Feiffer and made a bitter laughing noise in the back of his throat.

It was Number One.

He stepped forward into the light so they could see him.

14

The acid from the giant glass vats was still bubbling into the zinc bath. Number One turned it off. It made a sizzling sound as it settled in the bath.

Dobbs said incredulously, 'You——?' He stared at Number One in disbelief. The muzzle of the sub-machine gun stayed pointed directly at his chest. Number One glanced down at Curry's body and flicked the muzzle of the gun at Feiffer's revolver. Feiffer holstered it.

Inspector Ming said, 'Dobbs, I asked you if in your little world wonders will never cease. I expect an answer.'

'You go to hell!'

'I expect an answer!'

'You go to hell!'

Feiffer glanced at the Sterling. It was cocked. The hands holding it were rock steady. He looked at Ming's eyes. They were on Dobbs. Ming said coldly, 'No, Dobbs, you're the one who's going to hell and I'm the dirty little Chink who's going to put you there——' He said, 'I'm going to chop you into dogmeat and send you straight to Perdition.' He said, 'I'm going to cut you to ribbons a bit at a time, and when it's over I'm going to spit on you——' He ordered, 'Call me a dirty little Chink!'

'You bloodywell are!'

'Oh, I am. That's right. That's what I am all right. I'm the dirty little Chink who outwitted you at every turn and blew your beautiful lovely little airport to shit!' Ming said, 'That's who I am. The dirty little Chink who gave all the orders to Curry here so he could order Number Two around—the dirty little Chink who employed a European to boss around a dirty little Chink because people like you had to believe that the big brain behind it had to be a European.' He said, 'There was a European behind it. It was Curry. He ordered that dirty little Chink, Number Two, around, and that suited you just fine.' He said, 'Feiffer here, Dobbs, suited you even better. Feiffer here, Dobbs, speaks perfect Cantonese so he just had to be a suspect. He was a European gone wrong because he speaks Chink lingo, Dobbs. He had to be a prime suspect. It had to be him!' Inspector Ming said, 'Dobbs, it was me! Under your nose at the airport saying, "Yes, Mr Dobbs, no, Mr Dobbs"—it was me!' He said suddenly evenly to Feiffer, 'Mr Feiffer, you may wonder about the proficiency of my English. It is due entirely to the fact that Mr Dobbs here, after near enough to twenty years in the Colony, has never lowered himself to learn or retain more than two words in Chinese.' He said, 'All Mr Dobbs' Chinese staff speak perfect accentless English or Mr Dobbs' Chinese staff don't get promotion.' He said, 'I'm at the top. I'm actually an Inspector. Munday, the Chief Inspector, hasn't half my experience or half my intelligence, but he's a Chief Inspector. But then, Mr Munday is a White Man.' He said, 'I'm at the top now all right—for a Chink!' He turned to Dobbs and suddenly shouted, 'Dobbs, this is China! Hong Kong is in China!' He said, his voice just as quickly cold again, 'Dobbs, I'm going to kill you and just for good measure I'm going to lay the responsibility for all the killings right on your front doorstep.' He said to Feiffer, 'One of the advantages of working at the airport is the easy availability of forged passports. You simply let someone carrying one in or out go through in return for the information where he got it.' He said, 'That collection of rubbish in Curry's cupboard: the Swiss passport and the papers, they were all from me. There was no chance I was ever going to let him use them, but at the time of his usefulness they made him feel secure enough to get on with the job.' Ming said, 'Number Two never even knew of my existence. After the money was delivered I was simply going to kill Curry and let Number Two take the entire blame for everything.' He said to Dobbs, 'That would have suited everyone: the dumb Chink who passed the money over to the European mastermind, killed him, and then was too stupid to find out where the mastermind had hidden the money.' He said to Feiffer, 'You were perfect as the red herring. Putting you in Court would have made Dobbs the local sleuth of the century.' He said to Dobbs, 'Not bad for a Chink, Dobbs, is it?' He said with vehemence, 'Dobbs, people like you make me puke!'

Feiffer glanced at the single small window on the far wall. There was a sheer drop of three floors to solid concrete. 'My people are outside.'

'Yes, I know they are.' Ming said, 'And as soon as they hear the shots they'll move Heaven and Earth to smash their way in. By which time, I'll be upstairs in the generator room, from where, at the appropriate moment, I'll just saunter down and join them and say I came up after I heard the call on my car radio. In fact, I was just across the road busily making telephone calls.' He said, 'As soon as they find Dobbs' body Kai Tak will have this place swarming.' He said, 'And Dobbs, no one will ever notice just another Chink. Will they?'

Dobbs said, 'Superintendent Dobbs to you, you yellow scum!'

'Mr bloody Ming to you!' Ming said to Feiffer, 'If you're wondering how I managed to keep Curry's blood off my uniform, I wore my good old regulation raincoat.' He said, 'It's in the acid bath where Curry would have been.' He said, 'Where incidentally the clothes from the sewer trash went.' He said, 'I was just going to kill Curry and run.' He said coldly, 'Having you turn up, Dobbs, was a real bonus.'

Dobbs said, 'You won't get away with it.'

'I have got away with it! When they find you there'll be so much confusion no one will know what to do with themselves for weeks. Then I'll just ring up about the last device and take the money.' He said, 'I'll just say I'm one of the underlings who planted it. They'll find Feiffer shot with the machine gun and you with bullets from Feiffer's gun here.' He said, 'A nice classic shoot-out between the good guy and the bent cop. Simple!' He said to Feiffer, 'I'm sorry you have to go too, but you have to.' He said, 'In your case, I'll make it quick and painless.'

'That's very gracious of you, I'm sure.' Feiffer said, 'And by the way, thank you most sincerely for setting me up.'

'I'm sorry about that.'

'I'll just bet you are!'

Ming said, 'No, really, I am. I—'

'You killed over ninety people! Don't you hand me all this about mass murder justifying that good old Chinese re-establishment of importance bit! You're nothing but a murderer and a thief of any colour or bloody background!' He said, 'So don't you tell me you're going to do me any favours! You're the one to make people puke, not Dobbs! At least Dobbs doesn't kill people!'

'Piece by piece, he was killing *me*!'

'My heart bleeds for you!'

Ming said, 'Mr Dobbs, you stand over there by the bath.' He looked at Feiffer, 'Maybe you're right.' He said coldly, 'In which case, there's no point in wasting any more time on it.'

Dobbs said sarcastically, *'Number bloody One . . .'*

Ming said, 'Get over by the bath!'

*

The driver from the Emergency Unit got the back of his Land-Rover open. It was full of tear gas guns and carbines. O'Yee said, 'The heavy cutting gear!' He reached inside and wrenched at the steel box containing it. He shouted to the two Inspectors setting up their sniper rifles, 'The cutting gear! Chop down the doors!'

He wrenched at the steel box and shouted to Auden, 'Give me a hand, will you!'

*

Dobbs looked quickly around the room. His eyes met Feiffer's. He saw the window. He touched his revolver holster and frowned. Dobbs said slowly to Ming, 'Look—this place doesn't mean anything to me . . .' He raised his hand like a traffic policeman to stop him, 'Look—what the hell do I care about this place? Look—it isn't worth being killed for is it?'

Ming smiled.

'All this stuff about the Chinese is just a load of shit . . . you know it is . . .' He jerked his hand to Feiffer. 'Even he knows it is. All you want is the money.' Dobbs said suddenly loudly, 'Well, I'm the one who can get it for you! I can get the money! I can get *double* what you want! Why kill anyone for peanuts when you can get double?' He said cajolingly, 'Curry was the Principal. O.K. Fine. Everyone knows that. O.K. Fine. Then leave it like that—what the hell do you care? Well? I ask you, what do you care?' There was a movement of a muscle below his eyes. 'Well? What do you care? Why not?'

Feiffer said, 'Shut up, Dobbs.'

'You shut up! What the hell do you want to do? Die here over a few dead airplane passengers? What the hell does anyone else in the civilised world care what happens in some dirty little second-rate Colony in the middle of nowhere?' Dobbs said, 'You know why people come here, Feiffer! They come here to get what they can and then get out again as rich as hell!' He demanded from Ming, 'Isn't that right!'

Ming had a strange smile on his face.

Dobbs said, 'All this stuff I said about Chinks—you know I didn't mean all that! If I did mean it, I was wrong! I mean, other Chinks! I didn't mean people like you! If you'd told me you were planning something like this, I could have helped you! I can still help you!'

'How?'

'I can cover for you! We can say we found Feiffer in the act of killing Curry but that one of the others involved got away! We can say later that someone telephoned us for the money and then you can deliver it!' Dobbs said, 'You can deliver it to *us*! I can get us both on a plane to somewhere where there's no extradition in—in a bloody split second!' He said, 'With twice, maybe three times as much!'

'What about Feiffer?'

'What do we care about him?' Dobbs said, 'Look, I've been waiting all my life for an opportunity like this—' He said, 'Look, there's no need for you to do anything! I can kill him and we can say—' He said, 'We don't even have to lie about it! I'll admit I killed him! We can put a bit of blood on his clothing from Curry and say we caught him standing over—' Dobbs said, 'I can help you!' He began drawing his revolver very slowly and said, 'I'll prove it! I'll kill him for you now!' He glanced anxiously at the sub-machine gun, 'I'll move slowly! I'll only fire one shot! You can cover me!' The revolver came out of his holster carefully and stayed in Dobbs' hand. His finger was off the trigger. 'Look! I'll *unload* it! I'll only put one bullet in the gun so I couldn't possibly—' He snapped open the cylinder of the gun and emptied out five of the six cartridges. 'We can put the rest of the shells back in after he's dead!' He said to Ming, 'For God's sake, I don't want to die!'

Ming paused.

Dobbs said, 'It'll work! I know how it has to look!'

Ming's eyes stayed on the gun. It seemed to fascinate him.

Dobbs said, 'All right, so I'm a nothing!' His eyes blazed at Feiffer. He demanded, 'What did you expect?' He asked Ming, 'Yes?'

Ming paused. His eyes stayed on Dobbs and the one shell in the open chamber of the revolver. He seemed to be smiling.

Dobbs said, 'Look!' He spun the cylinder to put the cartridge out of alignment with the breech. 'I couldn't get a shot off anyway!'

The smile stayed on Ming's face. Feiffer glanced at him.

Dobbs said to Feiffer, 'Unload your gun!'

Feiffer flicked the six shells out into his open hand.

Dobbs said, 'I've spent the last eighteen years getting rich and you bloodywell know it, Ming, so why the hell shouldn't I want the big payoff? I don't like Chinks and that's too bloody bad, but so what?' He said, 'I care even less about some quasi-European like him! He's got nowhere to go! Well, I bloodywell have and so have you!' He said, 'Look, I don't like you one bloody bit and you hate my bloody guts—but between us we can make a bloody fortune! We can go our own ways—what the hell do I care if I never see you again?' He said, 'I can make it a mint! They'll believe me! You know they will!' He asked, 'Well? What about it?'

The smile stayed on Ming's face. Ming said, 'Nice try. As a matter of fact, I totally believe you.' He raised the sub-machine gun, 'But enough is enough.' His eyes stayed on the gun in Dobbs' hand. He said, 'Thanks for drawing your gun yourself. It makes it so much easier from a point of view of fingerprints.' He said, 'Dobbs you really aren't very much at all.' He lowered the gun for a second to glance at his watch to check the time.

He ducked automatically as both Feiffer and Dobbs threw their revolvers at the window simultaneously and went for the floor as a burst of machine gun fire lashed over their heads.

*

Auden had a tear gas gun in his hand in readiness as the Emergency Unit chopped at the door with the heavy cutting gear. He heard the glass go. Something came sailing out of a top window and hit the cement with a crash. He ran back down the steps and heard a quick burst of fire. O'Yee wrenched the gun from his hand and took a quick aim. He pressed the trigger.

There was a loud bang as the tear gas bomb smashed in through what was left of the window on the third floor.

*

There were pieces and sharp wood and mortar from the cupboards and walls flying about the room as it filled with gas. Feiffer reached out and felt Dobbs' arm. He pulled the arm and the arm came alive. Feiffer said, 'Out! This way!' as there was a short burst of fire and then a click. Curry's body was in his path. He shoved it out of the way and it disappeared into a thick cloud of gas settling on the floor. Tears began streaming down his face and his lungs constricted and choked as the gas came in. There was another click as Ming tried to clear the Sterling, then a chaos of coughing and then a clattering as he pulled the bolt back.

Feiffer's hand touched the door to the corridor. He pulled it open blindly and dragged Dobbs outside. Inside the room there was a long burst as Ming raked the floor searching for them. Feiffer slammed the door shut and got to his feet. He held the knob on the door tight shut. An explosion of wooden chips tore across the corridor as Ming sent a burst into the door, then there was a series of singing whines as the metal jacketed bullets ricocheted off the brass hinges and went arcing back into the room. Gas was coming out under the door into the corridor. Feiffer rammed his free hand into his coat pocket for the keys to the elevator. He found them. Another burst of fire came through the door, then stopped. There was a terrible fit of coughing as Ming tried to clear his lungs of the gas, then a final long burst from the gun as he turned in the room with his eyes blind and running.

There was a shattering of heavy glass. Feiffer heard it. He let go of the door and pulled at Dobbs against the wall. He shouted at Dobbs, 'Run like hell!'

Ming's eyes cleared. There was glass falling about him. Something had— Through the gas, for a split second, he saw a tidal wave of acid come cascading down at him from the six smashed hundred gallon vats.

He raised his arms as if to catch it.

15

The Commander's voice said on the phone, 'So what do you think about the possibility of there being a final device, Harry?' He said, 'After all, it's been two days and nothing's been found. What do you think?'

'What does Dobbs think?'

'I wasn't aware you two were such great friends these days.'

'We're not. Finding devices on airplanes is his affair.' Feiffer glanced at the wall clock. It was 6 p.m., time to think about going home. 'I don't see any reason to think that the late Inspector Ming wasn't a man of his word.'

'So you think there is a device?'

'I don't know. As I said, that's Dobbs' job.'

'Then you don't feel like going over to Kai Tak to give him some assistance?'

'No, I don't feel like going over to Kai Tak to give him some assistance.'

The Commander said placatingly, 'Look, Harry, I wouldn't like to be thought to be making excuses for people like Dobbs—'

'I'm very glad to hear it.'

'—but this business at Kai Tak resulted in absolute carnage. Surely you can appreciate that people are still worried about travelling on—'

'I just don't see how we can help, Neil. I think we've done our bit. Both Number Two and Ming talked about there being a last device, but what it is and where it is, I just don't know.

Surely to God Dobbs can take care of that himself. I don't see what else we can do here.'

'Dobbs tended to give the impression that he'd welcome your help any time you wanted to give it—'

'Tell him to get stuffed.'

'From what I gather from the reports, there's a strong possibility that he may even have saved your life up there in that room.'

'If that's true then he was only making amends anyway, so you'll understand if I don't appear to be too grateful.'

'Is that your last word on the matter?'

'My last word on the matter was to tell Dobbs to shove it.'

The Commander said, 'Well, it has been two days. That's longer than any of the others. Maybe it's gone wrong.'

'Sure.'

'We'll give it a week and see what happens.' The Commander said, 'If nothing's happened by then we'll assume it's all over.' He said pleasantly, 'Since it's just gone six I suppose you're looking forward to going home?'

Feiffer did not reply.

'O.K. then.' The Commander said, 'Enjoy yourself a bit more.' He said cheerfully, 'After all, it is Spring.' He said, 'You know, when I was your age—'

He heard a sharp click at the other end of the line and smiled to himself.

*

At 9 p.m. local time, the Chief Steward on El Al Flight Number 569 from Hong Kong to Delhi and Rome glanced at his watch. The aircraft was still out of the European zone and there was just time enough for the in-flight film before supper was served. He pushed the button on a wall console for the film to begin. Almost instantly, he stopped it and withdrew the cassette.

The plane was a charter flight full of American Rabbis on

their way to Europe and the Holy Land and an old 1955 film of Victor Mature starring in *The Egyptian* was not exactly the *Fiddler on the Roof* programme that had been scheduled.

The Chief Steward glanced anxiously at the nearest row of Rabbis. He noticed that the film was of the old nitrate kind and should not have been inserted into an in-flight cassette at all. He said unhappily, 'Someone goofed,' and went quickly towards the pilot's cockpit to have Rome radioed to have a replacement movie unstored and waiting.

He stopped for a moment and looked at the film. There was a tiny section chopped out of the first few feet of soundtrack and it would have jammed in the projector after the first few minutes anyway. He went back to the passenger seats and showed the film to the group of Chief Rabbis in the forward seats. The Rabbis kept their hands off it.

A thing like that—a movie about goddamned Egyptians on a good kosher Israeli airline, the first two Chief Rabbis thought, well, to say the least, it was—well, what could you say? Inflammatory?

The party of Rabbis opened their Talmuds and made good use of their extra time.

MORE MYSTERIOUS PLEASURES

HAROLD ADAMS
MURDER
Carl Wilcox debuts in a story of triple murder which exposes the underbelly of corruption in the town of Corden, shattering the respectability of its most dignified citizens. #501 $3.50

THE NAKED LIAR
When a sexy young widow is framed for the murder of her husband, Carl Wilcox comes through to help her fight off cops and big-city goons. #420 $3.95

THE FOURTH WIDOW
Ex-con/private eye Carl Wilcox is back, investigating the death of a "popular" widow in the Depression-era town of Corden, S.D. #502 $3.50

EARL DERR BIGGERS
THE HOUSE WITHOUT A KEY
Charlie Chan debuts in the Honolulu investigation of an expatriate Bostonian's murder. #421 $3.95

THE CHINESE PARROT
Charlie Chan works to find the key to murders seemingly without victims—but which have left a multitude of clues. #503 $3.95

BEHIND THAT CURTAIN
Two murders sixteen years apart, one in London, one in San Francisco, each share a major clue in a pair of velvet Chinese slippers. Chan seeks the connection. #504 $3.95

THE BLACK CAMEL
When movie goddess Sheila Fane is murdered in her Hawaiian pavilion, Chan discovers an interrelated crime in a murky Hollywood mystery from the past. #505 $3.95

CHARLIE CHAN CARRIES ON
An elusive transcontinental killer dogs the heels of the Lofton Round the World Cruise. When the touring party reaches Honolulu, the murderer finally meets his match. #506 $3.95

JAMES M. CAIN
THE ENCHANTED ISLE
A beautiful runaway is involved in a deadly bank robbery in this posthumously published novel.   #415 $3.95

CLOUD NINE
Two brothers—one good, one evil—battle over a million-dollar land deal and a luscious 16-year-old in this posthumously published novel.
#507 $3.95

ROBERT CAMPBELL
IN LA-LA LAND WE TRUST
Child porn, snuff films, and drunken TV stars in fast cars—that's what makes the L.A. world go 'round. Whistler, a luckless P.I., finds that it's not good to know too much about the porn trade in the City of Angels.
#508 $3.95

GEORGE C. CHESBRO
VEIL
Clairvoyant artist Veil Kendry volunteers to be tested at the Institute for Human Studies and finds that his life is in deadly peril; is he threatened by the Institute, the Army, or the CIA?   #509 $3.95

WILLIAM L. DeANDREA
THE LUNATIC FRINGE
Police Commissioner Teddy Roosevelt and Officer Dennis Muldoon comb 1896 New York for a missing exotic dancer who holds the key to the murder of a prominent political cartoonist.   #306 $3.95

SNARK
Espionage agent Bellman must locate the missing director of British Intelligence—and elude a master terrorist who has sworn to kill him.
#510 $3.50

KILLED IN THE ACT
Brash, witty Matt Cobb, TV network troubleshooter, must contend with bizarre crimes connected with a TV spectacular—one of which is a murder committed before 40 million witnesses.   #511 $3.50

KILLED WITH A PASSION
In seeking to clear an old college friend of murder, Matt Cobb must deal with the Mad Karate Killer and the Organic Hit Man, among other eccentric criminals.   #512 $3.50

KILLED ON THE ICE
When a famous psychiatrist is stabbed in a Manhattan skating rink, Matt Cobb finds it necessary to protect a beautiful Olympic skater who appears to be the next victim.   #513 $3.50

JAMES ELLROY
SUICIDE HILL
Brilliant L.A. Police sergeant Lloyd Hopkins teams up with the FBI to solve a series of inside bank robberies—but is he working with or against them?   #514 $3.95

PAUL ENGLEMAN
CATCH A FALLEN ANGEL
Private eye Mark Renzler becomes involved in publishing mayhem and murder when two slick mens' magazines battle for control of the lucrative market.   #515 $3.50

LOREN D. ESTLEMAN
ROSES ARE DEAD
Someone's put a contract out on freelance hit man Peter Macklin. Is he as good as the killers on his trail?   #516 $3.95

ANY MAN'S DEATH
Hit man Peter Macklin is engaged to keep a famous television evangelist *alive*—quite a switch from his normal line.   #517 $3.95

DICK FRANCIS
THE SPORT OF QUEENS
The autobiography of the celebrated race jockey/crime novelist.
#410 $3.95

JOHN GARDNER
THE GARDEN OF WEAPONS
Big Herbie Kruger returns to East Berlin to uncover a double agent. He confronts his own past and life's only certainty—death.
#103 $4.50

BRIAN GARFIELD
DEATH WISH
Paul Benjamin is a modern-day New York vigilante, stalking the rapist-killers who victimized his wife and daughter. The basis for the Charles Bronson movie.   #301 $3.95

DEATH SENTENCE
A riveting sequel to *Death Wish*. The action moves to Chicago as Paul Benjamin continues his heroic (or is it psychotic?) mission to make city streets safe.   #302 $3.95

TRIPWIRE
A crime novel set in the American West of the late 1800s. Boag, a black outlaw, seeks revenge on the white cohorts who left him for dead. "One of the most compelling characters in recent fiction."—Robert Ludlum.   #303 $3.95

FEAR IN A HANDFUL OF DUST
Four psychiatrists, three men and a woman, struggle across the blazing Arizona desert—pursued by a fanatic killer they themselves have judged insane. "Unique and disturbing."—Alfred Coppel.   #304 $3.95

JOE GORES
A TIME OF PREDATORS
When Paula Halstead kills herself after witnessing a horrid crime, her husband vows to avenge her death. Winner of the Edgar Allan Poe Award.   #215 $3.95

COME MORNING
Two million in diamonds are at stake, and the ex-con who knows their whereabouts may have trouble staying alive if he turns them up at the wrong moment.   #518 $3.95

NAT HENTOFF
BLUES FOR CHARLIE DARWIN
Gritty, colorful Greenwich Village sets the scene for Noah Green and Sam McKibbon, two street-wise New York cops who are as at home in jazz clubs as they are at a homicide scene.
                                        #208 $3.95

THE MAN FROM INTERNAL AFFAIRS
Detective Noah Green wants to know who's stuffing corpses into East Village garbage cans . . . and who's lying about him to the Internal Affairs Division.   #409 $3.95

PATRICIA HIGHSMITH
THE BLUNDERER
An unhappy husband attempts to kill his wife by applying the murderous methods of another man. When things go wrong, he pays a visit to the more successful killer—a dreadful error.   #305 $3.95

DOUG HORNIG
THE DARK SIDE
Insurance detective Loren Swift is called to a rural commune to investigate a carbon-monoxide murder. Are the commune inhabitants as gentle as they seem?   #519 $3.95

P.D. JAMES/T.A. CRITCHLEY
THE MAUL AND THE PEAR TREE
The noted mystery novelist teams up with a police historian to create a fascinating factual account of the 1811 Ratcliffe Highway murders.
                                        #520 $3.95

STUART KAMINSKY'S "TOBY PETERS" SERIES
NEVER CROSS A VAMPIRE
When Bela Lugosi receives a dead bat in the mail, Toby tries to catch the prankster. But Toby's time is at a premium because he's also trying to clear William Faulkner of a murder charge!   #107 $3.95

HIGH MIDNIGHT
When Gary Cooper and Ernest Hemingway come to Toby for protection, he tries to save them from vicious blackmailers. #106 $3.95

HE DONE HER WRONG
Someone has stolen Mae West's autobiography, and when she asks Toby to come up and see her sometime, he doesn't know how deadly a visit it could be. #105 $3.95

BULLET FOR A STAR
Warner Brothers hires Toby Peters to clear the name of Errol Flynn, a blackmail victim with a penchant for young girls. The first novel in the acclaimed Hollywood-based private eye series. #308 $3.95

THE FALA FACTOR
Toby comes to the rescue of lady-in-distress Eleanor Roosevelt, and must match wits with a right-wing fanatic who is scheming to overthrow the U.S. Government. #309 $3.95

JOSEPH KOENIG
FLOATER
Florida Everglades sheriff Buck White matches wits with a Miami murder-and-larceny team who just may have hidden his ex-wife's corpse in a remote bayou. #521 $3.50

ELMORE LEONARD
THE HUNTED
Long out of print, this 1974 novel by the author of *Glitz* details the attempts of a man to escape killers from his past. #401 $3.95

MR. MAJESTYK
Sometimes bad guys can push a good man too far, and when that good guy is a Special Forces veteran, everyone had better duck. #402 $3.95

THE BIG BOUNCE
Suspense and black comedy are cleverly combined in this tale of a dangerous drifter's affair with a beautiful woman out for kicks. #403 $3.95

ELSA LEWIN
I, ANNA
A recently divorced woman commits murder to avenge her degradation at the hands of a sleazy lothario. #522 $3.50

THOMAS MAXWELL
KISS ME ONCE
An epic *roman noir* which explores the romantic but seamy underworld of New York during the WWII years. When the good guys are off fighting in Europe, the bad guys run amok in America. #523 $3.95

ED McBAIN
ANOTHER PART OF THE CITY
The master of the police procedural moves from the fictional 87th precinct to the gritty reality of Manhattan. "McBain's best in several years."—*San Francisco Chronicle*.   #524 $3.95

SNOW WHITE AND ROSE RED
A beautiful heiress confined to a sanitarium engages Matthew Hope to free her—and her $650,000.   #414 $3.95

CINDERELLA
A dead detective and a hot young hooker lead Matthew Hope into a multi-layered plot among Miami cocaine dealers. "A gem of sting and countersting."—*Time*.   #525 $3.95

PETER O'DONNELL
MODESTY BLAISE
Modesty and Willie Garvin must protect a shipment of diamonds from a gentleman about to murder his lover and an *uncivilized* sheik.   #216 $3.95

SABRE TOOTH
Modesty faces Willie's apparent betrayal and a modern-day Genghis Khan who wants her for his mercenary army.   #217 $3.95

A TASTE FOR DEATH
Modesty and Willie are pitted against a giant enemy in the Sahara, where their only hope of escape is a blind girl whose time is running out.   #218 $3.95

I, LUCIFER
Some people carry a nickname too far . . . like the maniac calling himself Lucifer. He's targeted 120 souls, and Modesty and Willie find they have a personal stake in stopping him.   #219 $3.95

THE IMPOSSIBLE VIRGIN
Modesty fights for her soul when she and Willie attempt to rescue an albino girl from the evil Brunel, who lusts after the secret power of an idol called the Impossible Virgin.   #220 $3.95

DEAD MAN'S HANDLE
Modesty Blaise must deal with a brainwashed—and deadly—Willie Garvin as well as with a host of outré religion-crazed villains.
          #526 $3.95

ELIZABETH PETERS
CROCODILE ON THE SANDBANK
Amelia Peabody's trip to Egypt brings her face to face with an ancient mystery. With the help of Radcliffe Emerson, she uncovers a tomb and the solution to a deadly threat.   #209 $3.95

THE CURSE OF THE PHAROAHS
Amelia and Radcliffe Emerson head for Egypt to excavate a cursed tomb but must confront the burial ground's evil history before it claims them both.   #210 $3.95

THE SEVENTH SINNER
Murder in an ancient subterranean Roman temple sparks Jacqueline Kirby's first recorded case.   #411 $3.95

THE MURDERS OF RICHARD III
Death by archaic means haunts the costumed weekend get-together of a group of eccentric Ricardians.   #412 $3.95

ANTHONY PRICE
THE LABYRINTH MAKERS
Dr. David Audley does his job too well in his first documented case, embarrassing British Intelligence, the CIA, and the KGB in one swoop.
                                                          #404 $3.95

THE ALAMUT AMBUSH
Alamut, in Northern Persia, is considered by many to be the original home of terrorism. Audley moves to the Mideast to put the cap on an explosive threat.   #405 $3.95

COLONEL BUTLER'S WOLF
The Soviets are recruiting spies from among Oxford's best and brightest; it's up to Dr. Audley to identify the Russian wolf in don's clothing.
                                                          #527 $3.95

OCTOBER MEN
Dr. Audley's "holiday" in Rome stirs up old Intelligence feuds and echoes of partisan warfare during World War II—and leads him into new danger.   #529 $3.95

OTHER PATHS TO GLORY
What can a World War I battlefield in France have in common with a deadly secret of the present? A modern assault on Bouillet Wood leads to the answers.   #530 $3.95

SION CROSSING
What does the chairman of a new NATO-like committee have to do with the American Civil War? Audley travels to Georgia in this espionage thriller.   #406 $3.95

HERE BE MONSTERS
The assassination of an American veteran forces Dr. David Audley into a confrontation with undercover KGB agents.   #528 $3.95

BILL PRONZINI AND JOHN LUTZ
THE EYE
A lunatic watches over the residents of West 98th Street with a powerful telescope. When his "children" displease him, he is swift to mete out deadly punishment.   #408 $3.95

PATRICK RUELL
RED CHRISTMAS
Murderers and political terrorists come down the chimney during an old-fashioned Dickensian Christmas at a British country inn.

#531 $3.50

DEATH TAKES THE LOW ROAD
William Hazlitt, a universtiy administrator who moonlights as a Soviet mole, is on the run from both Russian and British agents who want him to assassinate an African general.

#532 $3.50

DELL SHANNON
CASE PENDING
In the first novel in the best-selling series, Lt. Luis Mendoza must solve a series of horrifying Los Angeles mutilation murders.

#211 $3.95

THE ACE OF SPADES
When the police find an overdosed junkie, they're ready to write off the case—until the autopsy reveals that this junkie *wasn't* a junkie.

#212 $3.95

EXTRA KILL
In "The Temple of Mystic Truth," Mendoza discovers idol worship, pornography, murder, and the clue to the death of a Los Angeles patrolman.

#213 $3.95

KNAVE OF HEARTS
Mendoza must clear the name of the L.A.P.D. when it's discovered that an innocent man has been executed and the real killer is still on the loose.

#214 $3.95

DEATH OF A BUSYBODY
When the West Coast's most industrious gossip and meddler turns up dead in a freight yard, Mendoza must work without clues to find the killer of a woman who had offended nearly everyone in Los Angeles.

#315 $3.95

DOUBLE BLUFF
Mendoza goes against the evidence to dissect what looks like an air-tight case against suspected wife-killer Francis Ingram—a man the lieutenant insists is too nice to be a murderer.

#316 $3.95

MARK OF MURDER
Mendoza investigates the near-fatal attack on an old friend as well as trying to track down an insane serial killer.

#417 $3.95

ROOT OF ALL EVIL
The murder of a "nice" girl leads Mendoza to team up with the FBI in the search for her not-so-nice boyfriend—a Soviet agent.

#418 $3.95

JULIE SMITH
TRUE-LIFE ADVENTURE
Paul McDonald earned a meager living ghosting reports for a San Francisco private eye until the gumshoe turned up dead . . . now the killers are after him.   #407 $3.95

TOURIST TRAP
A lunatic is out to destroy San Francisco's tourism industry; can feisty lawyer/sleuth Rebecca Schwartz stop him while clearing an innocent man of a murder charge?   #533 $3.95

ROSS H. SPENCER
THE MISSING BISHOP
Chicago P.I. Buzz Deckard has a missing person to find. Unfortunately his client has disappeared as well, and no one else seems to be who or what they claim.   #416 $3.50

MONASTERY NIGHTMARE
Chicago P.I. Luke Lassiter tries his hand at writing novels, and encounters murder in an abandoned monastery.   #534 $3.50

REX STOUT
UNDER THE ANDES
A long-lost 1914 fantasy novel from the creator of the immortal Nero Wolfe series. "The most exciting yarn we have read since *Tarzan of the Apes.*"—*All-Story Magazine.*   #419 $3.50

ROSS THOMAS
CAST A YELLOW SHADOW
McCorkle's wife is kidnapped by agents of the South African government. The ransom—his cohort Padillo must assassinate their prime minister.   #535 $3.95

THE SINGAPORE WINK
Ex-Hollywood stunt man Ed Cauthorne is offered $25,000 to search for colleague Angelo Sacchetti—a man he thought he'd killed in Singapore two years earlier.   #536 $3.95

THE FOOLS IN TOWN ARE ON OUR SIDE
Lucifer Dye, just resigned from a top secret U.S. Intelligence post, accepts a princely fee to undertake the corruption of an entire American city.   #537 $3.95

JIM THOMPSON
THE KILL-OFF
Luanne Devore was loathed by everyone in her small New England town. Her plots and designs threatened to destroy them—unless they destroyed her first.   #538 $3.95

DONALD E. WESTLAKE
THE HOT ROCK
The unlucky master thief John Dortmunder debuts in this spectacular caper novel. How many times do you have to steal an emerald to make sure it *stays* stolen?   #539 $3.95

BANK SHOT
Dortmunder and company return. A bank is temporarily housed in a trailer, so why not just hook it up and make off with the whole shebang? Too bad nothing is ever that simple.   #540 $3.95

THE BUSY BODY
Aloysius Engel is a gangster, the Big Man's right hand. So when he's ordered to dig a suit loaded with drugs out of a fresh grave, how come the corpse it's wrapped around won't lie still?   #541 $3.95

THE SPY IN THE OINTMENT
Pacifist agitator J. Eugene Raxford is mistakenly listed as a terrorist by the FBI, which leads to his enforced recruitment to a group bent on world domination. Will very good Good triumph over absolutely villainous Evil?   #542 $3.95

GOD SAVE THE MARK
Fred Fitch is the sucker's sucker—con men line up to bilk him. But when he inherits $300,000 from a murdered uncle, he finds it necessary to dodge killers as well as hustlers.   #543 $3.95

TERI WHITE
TIGHTROPE
This second novel featuring L.A. cops Blue Maguire and Spaceman Kowalski takes them into the nooks and crannies of the city's Little Saigon.   #544 $3.95

COLLIN WILCOX
VICTIMS
Lt. Frank Hastings investigates the murder of a police colleague in the home of a powerful—and nasty—San Francisco attorney.
#413 $3.95

NIGHT GAMES
Lt. Frank Hastings of the San Francisco Police returns to investigate the at-home death of an unfaithful husband—whose affairs have led to his murder.   #545 $3.95

DAVID WILLIAMS' "MARK TREASURE" SERIES
UNHOLY WRIT
London financier Mark Treasure helps a friend reaquire some property. He stays to unravel the mystery when a Shakespeare manuscript is discovered and foul murder done.   #112 $3.95

TREASURE BY DEGREES
Mark Treasure discovers there's nothing funny about a board game called "Funny Farms." When he becomes involved in the takeover struggle for a small university, he also finds there's nothing funny about murder.   #113 $3.95

■ ■